JUST A LITTLE DESIRE

NEW YORK TIMES BESTSELLING AUTHORS

Carly Phillips

Erika Wilde

Print Edition

Cover Photo: Wander Aguiar
Cover Design: Maria @steamydesigns

JUST A LITTLE DESIRE

I wasn't the type of woman who indulged in one-night stands, but the irresistible Liam Powers managed to charm me right into his bed—then disappeared before sunrise. I convinced myself the night was nothing more than a reckless lapse in judgment…until he walked into my office weeks later, looking every bit as sexy and confident as I remembered.

Only this time, Liam wasn't just the man who'd wrecked my self-control. He was the wealthy investor interested in saving my family's struggling tech company.

I told myself I could handle working with him. That I could ignore the spark between us and the way he looked at me. Like he still remembered every place on my body that he'd touched. I warned myself not to fall for that flirtatious smile a second time. Liam Powers didn't do relationships. And I didn't do heartbreak.

But partnership has a way of breaking down defenses. Late-night strategy sessions turned into banter and stolen glances. A business trip together had me falling into bed with him once more. Because Vegas revealed a softer, unexpected side of him—one that made me question everything I thought I knew about love, trust, and taking risks.

Then came Liam's secrets. His betrayal. And his revelation about someone I loved. And I had to decide whether to walk away…or believe in the man who was fighting for us with everything he had.

Because somewhere between enemies, lovers, and second chances, Liam Powers became the one thing I never expected…My future.

CHAPTER ONE

Liam

THE CLINK OF a fork against a champagne flute rang out across the ballroom, catching everyone's attention. Conversations faded, laughter dimmed, and two hundred heads turned toward the front of the room where the maid of honor stood beaming beside Fallon, the bride, who was also my new sister-in-law.

"Hello, everyone," the maid of honor said with cheerful enthusiasm. "For those of you who don't know me, I'm Brooke, Fallon's best friend. I've known her for a long time, and I can honestly say I've never seen her as happy as she's been since she met Noah."

I glanced down the table where I was seated as one of the groomsmen, my gaze shifting to my brother, Noah, as I absently swirled the champagne in my glass. His usually composed, uptight expression had softened. His eyes were on Fallon like she was the only thing in the room worth seeing. To him, she probably was. The free-spirited painter had cracked open something in my older brother that none of us knew was there. She'd been good for him. Anyone could see that, even a cynic like me.

That didn't mean I bought into the whole *happily ever after* narrative.

Brooke's speech went on, her voice growing more sentimental by the minute as she started waxing poetic about *soulmates* and *true love* and *finding your other half.* All the things I no longer believed in.

"Fallon and Noah might seem like opposites," Brooke said, her voice filled with affection, "but anyone who knows them can see they fit together perfectly. So, I'd like to raise a glass to my best friend and the one person in the world who completes her. To Fallon and Noah."

We all sipped our champagne, and I smirked at my other brother, Simon, in a way that communicated my skepticism. He shook his head, his mouth twitching as if he wanted to laugh but didn't dare. Smart man.

We were both groomsmen, but Noah had appointed his friend, Michael, as the best man because he hadn't wanted to choose between brothers. Whatever his reasons, I was grateful. Simon wasn't the sentimental speech type, and I certainly didn't believe in the forever kind of love that Brooke had talked about.

Still, I was genuinely happy for Noah. He adored Fallon, and while romantic love might not be for everyone, it brought out a side of him that was worth celebrating.

The best man's speech came next, mercifully shorter and far less emotional. He cracked a few well-aimed jokes about Fallon being the only person capable of removing the stick that Noah used to have up his ass, drawing laughter from everyone, then wished the couple well with a sincere smile.

Dinner resumed, which was gourmet and delicious. The whole wedding was a sophisticated affair. A jazz band set up in the corner of the room started playing soft, sultry notes that filled the space without overwhelming conversation.

"Lighten up," Simon said from beside me, nudging my arm. "You look like you're calculating the ROI on their marriage."

His comment was comical, because if there was anyone in the world that needed to *lighten up,* it was him. Simon was a grump most of the time, and I would know. He wasn't just my brother; he was my business partner in our investment firm—strategic, ruthless, brilliant, and a complete pain in the ass. I knew how controlling and cantankerous he could be, both in his personal life and in business. But our dynamic worked because we balanced each other out; his control-freak tendencies versus my easygoing pragmatism.

"You know weddings bring out the worst in me," I said, swirling the last of the champagne in my glass.

Understanding flashed in Simon's eyes. We didn't discuss what happened with Ivy. It was an unspoken rule in our family. My brother might have believed I was over it, but I doubted I ever would be. I hated how much power that one incident still had over me and my ability to commit again to any woman.

"It's been three years," Simon said quietly, his tone careful. Not pushing…just observing.

I stiffened. "I know how long it's been."

He was silent for a moment, then leaned back in his chair. "You don't have to stay for the whole reception, you know. Noah won't hold it against you."

I glanced at him, surprised. Simon wasn't usually one to give me an out. "Really? Mr. 'By the Book' is telling me I can bail?"

He shrugged. "I'm saying you've done your duty. Stood up for Noah at the ceremony, smiled for the photos, sat through dinner and the toasts." He paused, his voice dropping lower. "No one expects you to stay and torture yourself."

The understanding in his tone—rare for Simon—made my chest tighten. "I'm happy for him," I said and meant it. "I am. It's just…"

"Hard to watch," Simon finished when I didn't.

"Yeah."

He nodded slowly, studying me with those sharp, analytical eyes that missed nothing. "For what it's worth, not everyone gets their happy ending the first, or even second, time around. But that's not to say Noah doesn't deserve his."

"I know that." I set my glass down, jaw tightening. "I'm not that much of a bastard."

"Didn't say you were." Simon's mouth curved into something that almost resembled a smile. "But you're allowed to feel however you feel about it. Just maybe don't let Mom catch you sneaking out early. She'll guilt-trip you for the next six months."

That pulled a genuine laugh from me. "Noted."

"And Liam?" He waited until I met his eyes. "One bad investment doesn't mean you write off the whole market."

I stared at him for a beat, recognizing the business metaphor for what it was. "Sometimes it does," I said quietly.

Simon's expression shifted, something like disappointment crossing his features before he masked it. "Suit yourself. But you're better than this."

Before I could respond, the bride and groom's first dance was announced, effectively ending the conversation. I wasn't sure Simon was right, but I knew one thing with certainty. I wasn't ready to risk my heart again. Not now. Maybe not ever.

At that moment, Noah and Fallon stood and made their way to the dance floor, the jazz band's melody swelling into a romantic ballad. As I watched them, I couldn't help but think about the wedding I had once planned. Would I have looked at Ivy with the same besotted look that was on Noah's face as he twirled his smiling bride around the dance floor? Would I have felt that kind of certainty about my wife and our future if she hadn't left me just three weeks before our wedding?

Probably not.

Because happy women didn't cheat. They didn't walk away from a three-year relationship without a backward glance because they'd fallen in love with someone else while I'd been too wrapped up in my job on Wall Street to notice.

I forced the memories back, burying them where they belonged. Dwelling on the past did no good. It was over. Lesson learned and I'd moved on.

The first dance ended to warm applause and the floor quickly filled with other couples. Some guests mingled, family and old friends catching up while enjoying the atmosphere. Children ran around the back of the room, playing a game of tag, and a few people headed to the open bar.

I considered joining them for a stiffer drink to numb the edges, but what I really needed was a break from the wedding festivities, and hadn't Simon essentially given me permission to do so? No matter how I felt about the concept of weddings, I didn't want to ruin anyone's good time. Now that dinner and the speeches were over, I could slip out quietly. Escape the romance and sentiment before it suffocated me completely.

I remembered seeing a bar about a block away from the reception, so I stepped outside while everyone else was distracted. Standing right beside the entrance with her back leaning against the brick exterior of the building was my sister, Shannon. I knew she wasn't looking for an escape like I was. The vape pen in her hand and the smell of cotton candy in the air revealed her reason for stepping away from the party.

I stopped beside her, hands in my pockets. "You're

supposed to be inside celebrating."

She raised an eyebrow. "I could say the same to you. Where are *you* going?"

"Sneaking away," I admitted quietly, and rubbed a hand along the back of my neck. "Don't mention it to anyone."

She frowned. "It's Noah's wedding, Liam."

The guilt was instant. I looked back toward the doors, hearing the muffled, joyful sounds from inside, but the thought of Ivy, of the wedding I almost had, made it impossible to return.

"He won't even notice I'm gone," I said, forcing a shrug. "He's too wrapped up in wedded bliss. And I'm happy for him."

I hated how I sounded. This wasn't me. I wasn't the brooding type. Normally, I was the one making jokes, keeping things light. But today...even my normally easy charm felt like a lie.

Shannon tilted her head, studying me with the same quiet intensity Mom used when she knew one of us was lying. "You know, not every wedding has to remind you of her."

I exhaled on a groan. First Simon, and now my sister. "I'm fine."

"Liam—"

"I mean it, Shan." My voice came out sharper than I'd intended. "I'm happy for Noah."

She reached out, squeezing my arm. "I know you are. But you can be happy for him and still be hurt. Those things aren't mutually exclusive."

"I'm not hurt," I insisted. "It's been three years."

"Yeah, and you've dated half of Manhattan since then," she said bluntly. "And the second any woman wants something real, you bolt. That doesn't sound like someone who's moved on."

I looked away, jaw working. "I'm *not* having this conversation."

"Of course not," she said, wryly, then softened her tone. "I'm sorry. I'm not trying to be a bitch. I just…miss the version of you that actually believed in this stuff. The Liam who got excited about the future instead of running from it."

Her words hit harder than I'd expected and I swallowed against the tightness in my throat. "That version of me got his heart shredded," I said quietly. "I'm not going back to being that naïve. I'm happier this way. No attachments, no expectations, no one to disappoint when I don't live up to their expectations."

She sighed and took a pull from her vape pen. "Okay," she finally said, resignation in her voice. "Go. Get out of here. But, Liam, one day you're going to meet someone who makes you want to try again. And when that happens, don't let Ivy steal that from you, too. She's already taken enough."

I nodded, just to pacify her. "I'll keep that in mind."

"And I won't tell anyone you snuck out, unless Mom asks," she added, a knowing grin curving her lips. "You know she can sniff out a lie from us like a bloodhound."

I laughed. "You're the best."

"I know." She waved me off. "Now get out of here before I change my mind and drag you back inside to dance with Aunt Carol."

I grimaced. "You're evil."

"Sisterly love," she called after me as I headed down the sidewalk.

I shoved my hands deeper into my pockets as I walked, the sound of my shoes tapping against the concrete. The more distance I put between myself and the wedding reception, the easier it felt to breathe. The tightness in my chest loosened with each step.

Noah could have his happy ending. I was going to find that bar, order a shot of something strong, and find my own happy ending for the night. No strings, no promises, no heartbreak.

CHAPTER TWO

Morgan

THE BASS THRUMMED through me, a pulsing rhythm that made my body move without thought. I swung my hips to the beat, arms lifted above my head, hair brushing my shoulders as I danced and sang along with the music. Around me, my friends formed a loose circle, all of us laughing and dancing and having a great time under the glow of colored lights.

After a busy week at the office, I was letting go of the stress I'd been carrying over the possibility of investors stepping in to take control of the company my father had built from the ground up. GalvaTech wasn't just a business, it was my father's legacy and where I'd worked for years as a marketing director alongside my stepbrother, Parker, who was CTO of the company. We represented decades of hard work, innovation, and sacrifice. The thought of handing over even partial control to strangers who cared more about profit margins than the people who built the company into what it was, made my stomach turn.

But I refused to think about that right now. Tonight was about me celebrating my twenty-sixth birthday with friends and forgetting, just for a few hours, that the future of everything I cared about was hanging in the balance.

A man brushed up against me from behind as I danced, and a pair of large hands suddenly landed on my hips. I stiffened and spun around, my smile evaporating, telling him with my eyes that his advances were unwelcome. I wasn't opposed to being picked up in a bar, but I didn't like how presumptuous he was by getting handsy without even engaging in a flirty conversation first.

He raised his hands, still smiling. "Can't blame a guy for trying. Have a good night, Birthday Girl."

I almost asked how he knew, but then I remembered that I was wearing a glittery gold sash that proclaimed me the *Birthday Girl*. My best friend, Whitney, had draped it on me when we arrived. It clashed ridiculously with my short, sexy, body-hugging dress in a shade of green that matched my eyes, but I didn't care. I was having a great time and I didn't mind the attention. It made the night feel special.

"Come on," Becca, my sister-in-law, said in my ear, tugging me off the dance floor as the song changed. "Let's do another round of shots."

I laughed, breathless from dancing. "Just one more," I said.

We'd been here for a few hours, and I could already feel that perfect edge of a buzz. The warm, floaty kind that made everything lighter and happier. Too much more and I'd risk tipping into sloppy-drunk territory, which wasn't my goal. There was a fine line between remembering tonight as a good time and regretting my choices in the morning.

The bar was packed, typical for a Saturday, but we had managed to grab a table for all six of us when we arrived, and miraculously, no one had tried to steal it while we were dancing. We all gathered around the circular table while Becca headed to the bar to get our last round of shots, even though she was the only one that wasn't drinking alcohol tonight. At five months pregnant, it wasn't an option for her, but she didn't mind. In fact, she'd opened a tab so that she could pay for all the drinks and the appetizers we shared when we first arrived.

While Becca was at the bar, the rest of us chatted. Whitney sat right next to me, and she leaned in close with a smile on her face, her glossy, curly dark hair falling over one shoulder. "So, are you going to get that guy's number?"

She nodded in the direction of the dance floor, where the handsy man was still dancing, but his eyes were fixed our way. I considered her suggestion. He was good looking enough, with short blond hair and a smile that showed off perfectly straight, white teeth. But I didn't feel any spark or chemistry when our eyes met.

"I don't think so," I said, looking away from him.

"Well, there are plenty of other good-looking guys

here tonight," Whitney pressed, her tone playful but insistent. "And it's been a while since you dated anyone. Maybe you should try to pick someone up and have a little fun. Seriously, you look hot as hell."

I laughed, shaking my head. "Thanks, but I'm not going to hook up with someone just to say I did. You know me. I need more than that."

Whitney rolled her eyes good-naturedly. "Here we go."

"I'm serious," I said, leaning closer to be heard over the music. "I want the *real* thing. The butterflies. The spark. That pull in your chest that says, *this might actually mean something*. I'm not interested in sleeping with someone just to fill time or for an orgasm that my battery-operated boyfriend can handle just fine."

"God, you're such a hopeless romantic," she teased, smiling before taking a drink of her water.

I took no offense to her words. "I always have been. You know that."

Maybe too much so. I'd paid the price for that once before, falling for someone because I had misread the signals, convinced there was something more emotional between us than just sex, only to end up heartbroken. But I was still holding out for that special feeling. The butterflies. A relationship like my parents shared before Mom passed, and one like my father found again with Faith, his second wife.

I couldn't be mad or upset my father had moved on, not when he was so happy. Seeing him find that kind of love twice gave me hope that it was possible for me, too. I could admit though, at least to myself, the situation with James had definitely made me more cautious when it came to men and their motives.

Whitney's expression softened. "Yeah. But maybe holding out for *perfect* isn't doing you any favors."

I stilled, catching the shift in her tone, along with her reference to the guy I'd dated my senior year in college. "You're talking about James."

She hesitated, then nodded. "I just don't want you to close yourself off because of what happened with him. You haven't dated anyone seriously since and that was years ago, Morgan."

I glanced away from my friend's stare, the memory surfacing despite my best efforts to keep it buried. *James.* My college boyfriend, or at least I had thought he was my boyfriend. We'd spent months together. Late nights studying, long conversations, and the kind of sex that felt like it meant something. I'd fallen for him. Hard.

And then I found out he didn't feel the same way. I had faced rejection and humiliation all in one fell swoop and not only was I blindsided, but completely devastated too.

"I thought we had something real," I said, meeting her gaze again. "He told me he wasn't looking for anything serious, but I didn't believe him. I thought if I just waited, if I was patient enough, he would change his mind. That he'd realize he loved me, too." God, I'd been such a fool.

Whitney reached out, squeezing my hand. "I know."

"But he didn't." I forced a smile, even though the old hurt still stung. "He met someone else. Fell for her in, like, two weeks. Suddenly, he was ready for serious. Just not with me."

"He was an idiot," Whitney said fiercely.

"And I was just a convenient hook-up." I'd also spent way too much time wondering why *I* hadn't been good enough for him, beyond what I now recognized as regular booty calls. "Either way, I learned my lesson. I'm not going to chase after someone who doesn't feel the same way about me. And I'm not going to settle for less than I deserve just because I'm afraid of getting hurt again." But I also wasn't a serial dater and didn't want to waste my time with someone I had no chemistry with.

Whitney sighed, resting her chin on her hand. "I get that. I do. I just don't want to see you close yourself off completely. You have these insanely high standards, and I'm worried you're going to miss out on someone great because you're too busy looking for those fireworks right away."

I considered her words. Whitney had known me since freshman year in high school, and she had a knack for cutting straight to the heart of things in a way only a best friend could. Maybe she was right. It was hard to admit that I had a bad habit of overthinking when I looked for romantic partners. I had to wonder if I'd passed up opportunities for a genuine connection because I was too hung up on looking for a man that ticked all my boxes right away. Maybe I was missing out on what could be something special because I was too wary of trusting a man and his true intentions.

"I'll think about it," I finally said, because I didn't know what else to say.

She smiled, bumping her shoulder against mine. "That's all I wanted to hear and I don't mean to give you a hard time. I just want you to be happy. I know you've always hoped to find true love, and I want to see that happen for you."

Something in my chest softened and I smiled back at her. "I appreciate that, and you. Really."

Just then, Becca returned to the table with a waitress following her, who was holding a tray of Fireball shots and one glass of what looked like a soda for Becca. My sister-in-law looked flustered, her cheeks red and her shoulders slumped. Something was wrong.

"Hey, what's going on?" I asked Becca as the waitress set the drinks on the table.

Becca bit her bottom lip and pulled me aside so that we were out of earshot of the others. "It's so embarrassing. My card was declined when I tried to close out the tab. I have no idea why. I need to call Parker. You know he handles all our finances. Maybe something's up with the account."

I nodded, trying to reassure her. Parker, my stepbrother, was a computer genius with a knack for numbers. He managed their bills and investments and kept their household running smoothly. If there was an issue, he'd figure it out.

"I'm sure it's just a mistake," I said gently. "Do you want me to pay the bill for now?"

Her eyes widened and she quickly shook her head. "No way," she said, looking even more embarrassed. "I don't want you to pay the bill on your birthday. This was going to be my treat."

"I know," I said, placing a hand on her arm. "But really, Becca, it's not a big deal. If you're that worried about it, you can pay me back later, okay?"

She hesitated, pride clearly warring with practicality before she sighed. "Okay, fine. But I *will* pay you back."

We returned to the table long enough to take our shots. Whitney lifted hers, eyes sparkling. "To Morgan!"

"To Morgan!" everyone echoed, their voices overlapping in laughter.

The Fireball's cinnamon burn slid down my throat, warm and sweet, chasing away the last traces of work stress and old heartbreak. "I'll be right back." I set my empty glass down and grabbed my purse.

I headed to the bar to settle the bill, weaving through the crowd. The DJ had just taken a break, so people from the dance floor were gathering around, trying to grab fresh drinks before the music started again.

I slid into an open space at the end of the bar, sandwiched between a couple who couldn't keep their hands off each other and a man who looked overdressed for a random bar. His tuxedo jacket hung on the back of his bar stool. His crisp white shirt was open at the throat, sleeves rolled up to his forearms, and his black tie hung loose around his neck. His dark brown hair was thick and styled back off his forehead, and the faintest shadow of stubble darkened his jaw.

He was sexy as hell and looked like trouble in the best possible way. And when his eyes flicked toward me, skimming me from head to toe, it felt like a physical touch. My skin tingled everywhere his intense gaze lingered.

"Can I help you?" the bartender asked, jolting me out of my daze.

I pulled my eyes away from the gorgeous, formally dressed man. "Uh, yes. My friend just tried to pay our tab and had a little trouble—"

"I took care of that," a smooth, deep, masculine voice said from beside me.

I turned back to Mr. Tuxedo in surprise. "What?"

"I paid the woman's tab," he said easily. "She looked upset, so I told the bartender to put it on my card."

The bartender gave a quick nod of confirmation. "Your bill is paid in full," he said, before moving down the bar to take a drink order.

"Oh." I blinked at the man, shocked by his random generosity. "Thank you. You didn't have to do that."

He gave a slight shrug, the movement drawing my attention to the strong line of his shoulders. "It's not a big deal."

His smile reached his eyes, warm and disarming. They were a mesmerizing copper color, and I wanted to stare into them endlessly. I also didn't miss the genuine interest in his gaze as he stared back.

And just like that, something fluttered in my chest. The kind of instantaneous spark I'd been telling Whitney I wanted to feel.

"It *is* a big deal," I said, trying to sound composed even as my pulse sped up. "That tab was probably huge. Let me pay you back."

The couple beside us moved away from the bar, freeing up a stool. He gestured toward the now vacant seat with an inviting, flirtatious smile. "How about you have a drink with me instead. Then, we'll call it even."

It wasn't a question. Not quite. But the way he said it—calm, certain, like he already knew I'd say yes—sent a little thrill through me.

I should have hesitated. Should have at least thought about it for more than half a second. But Whitney's voice echoed in my head. *Maybe if you stopped expecting fireworks right away, you'd give someone a real chance.*

Except I *was* feeling a spark. The second his eyes met mine, there had been no doubt in my mind that the awareness between us had been mutual.

Maybe Whitney and I were both right. I needed to open myself up to new experiences with men without over-analyzing the situation, but it didn't hurt that I felt such an immediate connection with this gorgeous man who'd just offered to buy me a drink.

He was confident and direct and left the choice

entirely up to me. I could say no, thank him again for covering our tab, and walk away. Go back to my friends and spend the rest of the night wondering *what if.*

Or I could stay and see where things might lead.

My heart gave a decisive thump, making the decision for me.

"I'd love to," I said, sliding onto the stool next to him.

His gaze followed the movement, tracking the way my dress rode up slightly as I settled onto the seat, then along the curve of my waist, the fullness of my breasts, and even the sway of my hair as I settled in.

When his eyes finally came back to mine, there was an unmistakable heat and desire there that made it impossible to remember what I'd just said, because I felt it, too.

With that one look, the night shifted, thick with the kind of anticipation that made the air hum with promise, along with the certainty that whatever *this* was, it wasn't going to be just another drink.

What better way to end my birthday celebration than by tempting fate with the sinfully good-looking man beside me?

CHAPTER THREE

Liam

"WHAT'S YOUR DRINK of choice?" I asked the beautiful woman perched on the stool beside me.

When I paid the pregnant woman's tab a few minutes earlier, I hadn't thought twice about it. She looked frazzled and upset, so when she walked away, promising to return with a different method of payment, I'd been compelled to give the bartender my credit card. It was a little pricey, but that didn't matter. My pockets were deep and I figured the small act of decency had been a nice way to balance the scales and assuage my guilt after walking out on Noah's wedding reception.

But meeting *her*? That was pure, unexpected luck.

Her green dress hugged her curves like it had been made for her stunning figure. Her dark hair brushed her shoulders as she turned toward me, eyes bright with amusement. "I'll have Sex on the Beach," she said.

I raised an eyebrow, a grin tugging at the corners

of my mouth. "That's bold. Not that I'm objecting."

She laughed, the soft and lilting sound cutting right through the bar noise. "It's a drink with peach schnapps, vodka, and orange juice," she clarified, still smiling.

I signaled the bartender to come back over and ordered her girly drink. I still had a glass of bourbon in front of me that I'd been sipping on since I arrived.

"I'm Liam," I said, introducing myself while the bartender started mixing her cocktail.

"Morgan," she replied.

She extended her hand and I grasped it in mine, feeling that undeniable jolt of awareness settling deep and low. I didn't let go right away. Neither did she. Her skin was warm and soft, and my mind immediately went to imagining what it would be like to feel those slim fingers gliding over my bare skin, or stroking my cock. My dick twitched at the thought.

Finally, she slipped her hand free and tucked a strand of silky hair behind her ear, that small, feminine motion drawing my gaze to the graceful curve of her neck before I focused back on her face.

"So, what's a beautiful woman like you doing in a place like this, besides turning heads?"

She laughed at my deliberately cheesy pickup line, a soft shade of pink sweeping across her cheeks at the compliment. "Escaping work stress mostly, but tonight's about fun." She tipped her head, her gaze taking in my attire. "What about you? Tux says wedding, but sitting in a bar like this, you look like you're hiding from whatever formal affair you left behind."

Her tone was playful, but her eyes, bright and assessing, lingered just long enough to make my pulse stir. "I'm actually skipping out on my brother's wedding reception, which is, as we speak, still going on just down the street," I said, surprising myself by admitting the truth. "I needed a break from all the 'happily ever after' vibes. But running into you? Best part of the night so far."

Her eyes widened in shock as she latched on to the first part of my reply. "You actually ditched your *brother's* reception?"

I gave her a small, rueful wince. "Guilty."

"Please tell me you at least stayed for the cake cutting," she said, amusement dancing in her eyes.

I shook my head, enjoying her quick wit and bubbly personality. "I'm afraid not."

Her jaw dropped, her expression exaggerated and charmingly dramatic. "That's just criminal. The cake is *the best part* of any wedding. Then again, I just love cake in general and any excuse to eat it."

I couldn't help the grin that tugged at my mouth. I found everything about her infectious, and I could feel the mutual attraction sparking across the inches of space between us. In the shifting light of the bar her green eyes sparkled like polished glass, and I found myself drawn to the glimmer of mischief in them.

"I'm guessing you're the birthday girl," I said, my gaze sliding to the glittery sash draped across her full breasts. Her sexy-as-hell dress was cut low enough to show off mouth-watering cleavage. This woman had curves for days, the kind of lush body I could easily imagine losing myself in for hours.

"Yep," she said, accepting her drink from the bartender. "I'm twenty-six today."

"Twenty-six," I repeated, letting my eyes drift over her again, slower this time, taking in the fact that she was six years younger than me. Not that it mattered in a situation like this, which for me was always an uncomplicated and temporary distraction. "Was twenty-five a good year for you?"

She took a sip of her drink, considering the question. "It's been…complicated. But tonight? Tonight's been perfect so far."

The way she said the words, the way her gaze held mine, made the attraction between us much stronger. "Complicated how?" I asked, genuinely curious.

She shrugged, but I caught the brief flash of tension in her shoulders. "Work stuff. Family business. Lots of pressure and decisions that feel too big for one person to make." She paused, then seemed to shake it off, her smile returning. "But I'm not thinking about any of that tonight. Tonight, I'm just…letting loose."

"Dangerous mindset," I teased, lowering my voice slightly. "Letting loose on your birthday."

She gave me a flirtatious grin. "Maybe I like a little danger."

Fuck. That sent a surge of heat straight through me.

"So, what about you?" she asked, leaning in just

enough that I caught the faint scent of her perfume, something warm and subtly floral. "Why are you really hiding out in a bar instead of celebrating with your brother and family? Anxiety about weddings in general, or just his?"

I huffed a quiet laugh, impressed by how quickly she'd read between the lines. "Let's just say weddings bring up some…unpleasant memories for me," I found myself sharing as I leaned in a bit closer, so our knees brushed under the bar. "Figured I'd spare everyone my cynicism and grab a drink instead."

"Ahh." Understanding flickered across her face. "Bad breakup?"

I hesitated, wondering why it was so easy to open up and talk to her, a virtual stranger, when this was a topic I avoided like the plague. "Something like that." I took a sip of my bourbon, letting the burn ground me before I revealed the rest. "Three years ago, my ex-fiancée ended things three weeks before the wedding."

Her expression softened. "Ouch. That's brutal." She lifted her glass toward mine. "Sounds like we both needed this escape. To unexpected meetings?"

I clinked my glass to hers. "To that, and to making the night even more memorable."

She grinned and placed the straw in her mouth to take a sip, drawing my eyes to her lips. The bottom was plump, soft-looking, and all I could think about was how it would feel caught between my teeth, not to mention a few other sinful things I could do to that luscious mouth.

Damn. When was the last time a woman made me feel like this? It wasn't just lust, though there was plenty of that. It was the way she carried herself that drew me in. Confident, but playful without trying too hard. The kind of woman who didn't need attention, but drew it effortlessly. There was an energy about her, something magnetic that got under my skin before I knew it was even happening.

She made me feel…*something* again. Like that dull, cold indifferent world I'd been living in since Ivy walked out on me suddenly had a pulse again, and that rhythm beat in time with Morgan's easy laughter, her warm, lilting voice, and the subtle, natural sway of her body toward mine. It was like I'd walked out of the wedding in search of something…and here she was.

The thought startled me, how easily she'd slipped beneath my defenses. I needed to shift gears before I did something reckless, like find out if her lips tasted as sweet as they looked.

"So," I said, smiling at her as I continued our playful conversation. "Did you get anything good for your birthday?"

She tilted her head, toying with the straw between her fingers. "Well, a handsome stranger bought me and my friends a bunch of drinks and appetizers."

"Handsome, huh?" I arched a brow. "Sounds like a guy with impeccable charm."

Her lips curved, the teasing glint in her eyes unmistakable. "Or maybe he just likes rescuing damsels in distress."

"Maybe," I murmured, holding her gaze. "Though I don't see a damsel in distress anywhere near me. Just a woman who knows exactly how to handle herself."

That earned me a quiet laugh, the feminine sound curling around my senses. "Careful, Liam," she said softly. "You might make a girl think you're flirting."

"And what if I am?" I asked huskily.

Her lashes fluttered once, the corner of her mouth lifting in a way that pulled me in deeper. "Then I'd have to say you're doing a pretty good job of it."

Before I could stop myself, I reached out and brushed my knuckles down her arm, feeing the subtle tremor that ran through her at my touch. Her skin was warm, smooth, and the way she didn't pull away sent a jolt straight to my cock. "Then I'll take that as a sign I should keep going," I said in a low voice that didn't hide my desire one bit.

"Maybe you should," she murmured, her eyes locking on mine as she took another sip of her drink.

So, I did, my next question purposely shifting into more intimate territory. "Do you have any other birthday wishes?" I dared to ask.

Her teeth grazed her bottom lip before she replied. It was slow, deliberate, like she knew exactly what it did to me. Heat pooled low in my body, my cock aching in anticipation of where this encounter could lead.

"I might," she admitted, her gaze holding mine.

"If you say it out loud, I might make it come true." I winked at her, but my tone was serious, edged with the promise of following through.

She smiled, arching a brow. "You sound pretty confident for someone who ditched a wedding tonight."

"Maybe I needed something better to celebrate," I said honestly, shocking myself by letting a little more of my guard drop. "And I think I just found it. Meeting you feels like a fresh start, even if it's just for tonight and fulfilling your birthday wish." Because for me, that was all it could be and I needed her to know that right up front.

Her breath hitched, the rise and fall of her chest subtle but impossible to miss. "You don't even know what I want."

"I can make an educated guess," I said, tracing the rim of my bourbon glass with a fingertip.

"Yeah?" She tilted her head to the side, a challenge sparking in her eyes. "What do you think my wish is?"

Meeting her gaze directly, I boldly lowered my hand to her knee, resting my palm on the soft, warm skin of her thigh where the hem of her dress ended, and took a risk. "I don't think you're ready for the night to end. You want something you'll still be thinking about tomorrow, maybe longer. It would be my pleasure to give you that."

I brushed my thumb along the inside of her thigh, and her lips parted on a soft exhale. The noise of the bar faded. The music, laughter, everything. All I saw was her and the mutual desire darkening her eyes.

"And if I said I was tempted by your offer?" she asked seductively.

"Then I'd say let me show you how good temptation can feel." My thumb traced another slow circle against her skin, aching to get her alone so I could follow through on the promise and explore every secret her body had to offer.

I pulled back just enough to meet her eyes again, and for a moment neither of us moved as we stared at one another. The air between us pulsed with possibilities—charged, reckless, and already past the point of pretending this was just flirting. The low lighting in the bar painted soft gold across her skin, and in that moment, I didn't give a damn about the wedding, the guilt, or the emotional wreckage Ivy had left in her wake.

Just Morgan. And the possibility of what came next. Of her naked and writhing beneath me while I completely ruined her. I wanted to lose myself in her warm, willing body and draw out every shiver, every moan, and feel her shatter around my cock.

And I wanted to take my time doing it.

I opened my mouth to ask if she wanted to get out of here, but before I could a woman with glossy black curls and a short black dress appeared next to Morgan, breaking the charged silence between us.

"Hey, I wondered where you'd gone," the woman said to Morgan. Her gaze flicked toward me, but didn't linger. "Everything okay?"

"Yeah," Morgan said easily as she finished her cocktail. "Liam here offered to buy me a birthday drink."

"Oh, that was nice." The woman glanced between us again, her expression uncertain. "We were about to head out, but we can wait until you're done."

Morgan shook her head, her gaze cutting to mine. Those green orbs were captivating and allowed me to see every emotion she was feeling. The woman was an open book, and she clearly wanted me just as much as I wanted her.

"No, you don't have to do that," she said, glancing back at the other woman with a reassuring smile. "You guys can go ahead and leave."

"Are you sure?" her friend asked. "Becca's the designated driver."

"I'm sure," Morgan insisted. "I'll get an Uber home."

Her friend looked at me again, warily, her brows drawn together. I had to respect that. She was being protective of her friend.

"Don't worry, Whit," Morgan said, a slight smile on her lips. "I'm taking your advice. I'm not wasting my time."

I didn't know what that meant, but her friend clearly did. The guarded look on her face cleared and she nodded. "Okay. But I want you to text me later so that I know you're safe."

The two women hugged and her friend walked away, joining a group that included the pregnant woman whose card was declined. A soft touch on my arm brought my attention back to Morgan, who was leaning toward me again with a very sensual smile on her face.

"What do you think about getting out of here?" she asked.

My pulse kicked hard. I already wanted her, but there was something about the confidence in her tone, the certainty, that lit up every nerve inside me. A bold woman was hot as hell, and I always appreciated one who knew what she wanted and didn't hesitate to ask for it.

"There's a hotel across the street," I said, my voice rougher than I'd intended. I'd noticed it earlier on my walk to the bar. It was close, convenient, and right now, the only option that didn't involve waiting.

Morgan slid off her stool, standing so close that I could feel the heat of her body and inhale that intoxicating scent of jasmine and vanilla.

"Then let's go," she murmured.

It was the only invitation I needed. I closed out my tab and grabbed her hand, leading her out of the bar and into the night.

Whatever this evening turned into, I already knew one thing for certain. For tonight, Morgan was mine, and I was going to enjoy every single second of fucking her.

CHAPTER FOUR

Morgan

THE HOTEL EXUDED understated luxury, with gleaming marble flooring in the lobby along with brass and mahogany accents throughout. I caught sight of a bar, and I could hear piano music drifting from the lounge, but Liam and I weren't interested in another public setting. With my hand in his, we headed straight to the check-in desk.

He surprised me by asking for the best suite they had. I didn't argue. If he wanted to spend a fortune on a hotel room for just one night, who was I to stop him?

The room was on the top floor and certainly extravagant, with a massive king-sized bed and floor-to-ceiling windows that offered a breathtaking view of the city. New York was truly amazing, I sometimes forgot how alluring it could be since I'd lived here my entire life. But seeing it from this point of view, with tall buildings lit up against the night sky, I was awed by the splendor of it all.

Liam crossed to a small sitting area and picked up

the laminated room service menu on a round table by the sofa and perused the offerings. "Ah, yes. This is perfect."

He picked up the phone before I could ask what he was talking about and pressed a button.

"Do you still have room service available?" he asked the person on the other end of the line. "Great. Please send up a slice of cake." He glanced back at me and asked, "Vanilla or chocolate?"

"I…umm, chocolate."

He repeated my preference into the phone, then hung up.

I raised an eyebrow at him. "You ordered me cake?"

He shrugged. "I thought it was only fitting that I treat you to a slice for your birthday since I know how much you like it." He grinned at me. "I pay attention, Morgan."

Yes, he did. His thoughtful gesture, and remembering a casual comment I'd made at the bar, created another little flutter, spreading a pleasant warmth through me. It wasn't just attraction, but something more…intimate. Definitely a moment of sincerity I hadn't expected from a stranger.

I slowly crossed the room to him, brushing my fingers along the smooth fabric of his tuxedo jacket before sliding my hands beneath the lapels and splaying my palms on his firm chest. He was about a foot taller than me, so I had to tilt my head back to look up at him.

"You really didn't have to do that," I said, though I was pleased that he had.

"Maybe not," he said in a low voice as his gaze dropped to my lips. "But I wanted to."

The air shifted, and something electric pulsed between us now that we were completely alone. Emboldened by the desire already coursing through me, I pushed his jacket off his shoulders and down his arms, never breaking eye contact as it landed on the carpet behind him with a muted thud.

His hands found my hips like it was instinct, his grip steady, certain, and warm. Unlike the man at the bar earlier while I'd been dancing, *this* claim was welcome. Liam's touch wasn't rushed or rough, though it *was* deliberate, like the way a confident man touched something he already knew was his.

He pulled me closer, his thumbs tracing slow circles through the fabric of my dress. The soft friction sent a rush of heat straight through me, tightening my nipples against the lace lining of my bra. My breath caught as our hips aligned and the warmth of his body pressed against me.

This close, his scent was darker. Smoky with a hint of bourbon, and something faint and clean, like rain on wood. I tipped my head back to meet his gaze, transfixed by the quiet intensity in the way he looked at me.

"You clearly *do* pay attention," I murmured, my voice barely above a whisper. "So what else have you noticed?"

A slow, seductive smile curved his lips. "That you're pretending to be calm and composed right now." His thumbs brushed higher along my waist. "And you're going to fucking love it when I make you lose control."

I laughed huskily as I slid my fingers up the front of his shirt, stopping just beneath the open collar. His pulse beat steady and strong, and I wanted to lean forward and run my tongue along the base of his neck just to taste his skin. "You're awfully sure of yourself," I said.

He smirked. "Oh, I'm definitely confident you'll have an orgasm or two before I'm through with you."

I couldn't suppress a shiver at his promise, or at the way one of his hands slid around to my back, then lower, cupping my ass in his palm. He dipped his head slightly toward mine, and my lips instinctively parted for him while anticipation swirled in my belly.

Before our lips connected, a sharp knock sounded at the door, shattering the seductive moment. I dropped my forehead against his chest, unable to stop the low, involuntary groan that slipped out before I could catch it.

Liam sighed in resignation. "Room service here has impeccable timing," he said in a dry tone.

He stepped back with obvious reluctance. The loss of contact was disappointing, leaving a chill where his body had been just moments ago. While he crossed the room I sat down on the couch. He opened the door, exchanged a few polite words with the man on the other side, then returned with a covered dish.

He set the plate on the small table in front of the sofa, sat down beside me, then lifted the silver dome with a flourish, revealing a large, single slice of chocolate cake. The scent was rich, dark, and decadent.

"Your dessert, Birthday Girl," he said with a grin.

I couldn't help but smile right back. "You're really going to make me eat cake before you kiss me?" I teased him.

His gaze dropped to my mouth, then slowly lifted back to my eyes. "Who said I couldn't do both?"

He let that promise hang in the air between us as he picked up the fork, cut off a small section, and lifted it to my lips. I let him feed me, and the first taste was an explosion of luscious flavor on my tongue. I moaned, turning the sweet moment into a sensual one. Liam's eyes darkened with desire as he continued feeding me a few more bites, the air between us thickening with sexual tension.

"Good?" he asked, his voice lower now, a bit rougher.

I nodded, my tongue darting out to catch a smear of chocolate at the corner of my mouth, very aware of how his gaze tracked the movement. "Better than good."

He looked pleased, like he'd gotten the exact reaction he wanted. "Then I think it's my turn to taste."

Instead of feeding himself a piece, he dragged his finger through the frosting and brought it to my bottom lip, spreading it slowly across.

My breath caught. "Liam—"

He didn't let me finish. His mouth was on mine before I could process what was happening, his tongue sweeping across my lip to taste the chocolate, and me. His claim wasn't gentle. Wasn't tentative. It was deliberate and consuming, and it made my head spin.

I made a sound, something between a gasp and a moan, and felt him respond immediately. His hand slid into my hair, angling my head exactly where he wanted it, while his other hand moved from my knee up my thigh, his palm hot on my skin.

I parted my lips, giving him access, and he deepened the kiss with a low sound that vibrated through his chest. He tasted of chocolate and bourbon, and it was completely my undoing. My fingers curled into the front of his shirt, needing something solid to hold onto as I pulled him even closer. The city outside blurred to nothing, a smear of light beyond the windows, and suddenly there was only the press of Liam's body and his dark, irresistible pull.

He didn't rush. He kissed like a man who understood the value of control and how to wield it. Each slow drag of his mouth against mine, intentional. Every sweep of his tongue told me he wasn't just chasing a reaction, he was learning all my subtle nuances.

That realization hit harder than it should have. He was a stranger. This was supposed to be simple pleasure, an escape, a night to remember. But there was something in the way Liam touched and kissed me that made it impossible to pretend it was something so casual. At least for me.

Focusing on the desire I couldn't deny, I arched into him, my breasts brushing his chest, seeking more of everything with this man. His kiss deepened, the rhythm shifting from patience to hunger, and the low sound he made against my lips sent a shiver racing down my spine.

My trembling fingers fumbled over the buttons of his shirt, eager to touch him. I managed to free a few before my hands flattened against his warm, smooth skin, my palms gliding over his broad chest and tracing his sculpted abs.

For a man who kissed with control, he burned hot beneath the surface. And for a woman who came here wanting just a hot, memorable night, I feared I was already in much deeper than I'd ever intended.

When he finally pulled back, we were both breathing hard.

"Christ," he muttered, his thumb brushing along my jaw. "I've been wanting to do that all night."

"Then why did you stop?" I asked breathlessly.

"Because if I keep kissing you on this couch, I won't be able to stop." His hand slid higher on my thigh, his thumb grazing across the front panel of my damp panties. "And when I finally get you out of this dress, I want to take my time."

Heat flooded through me, settling low in my belly. "Maybe I don't want you to take your time."

A slow smile curved his mouth. "Oh, you will." He

leaned in again, lips brushing across mine. "Trust me."

If that was the case, then he was right. I didn't want an uncomfortable couch for what he had in mind. I wanted that roomy, king-sized bed to spread out on.

I stood, reaching for his hand. "Come with me."

He followed without hesitation, the air between us vibrating with everything unspoken as I led him toward the bed. I slipped the *Birthday Girl* sash over my head and tossed it aside. I stepped out of my heels, then turned around and looked at him over my shoulder.

"Would you mind?" I asked, referring to my zipper.

Liam's eyes darkened as he moved closer and grasped the metal tab, placing a warm, damp kiss to my shoulder as he pulled the zipper down. He slipped the thin straps off my shoulders, allowing the dress to slide down my body and pool at my feet.

"Jesus, Morgan," he murmured, his voice rough and reverent as he came around to stand in front of me. "You're beautiful."

I was glad I'd worn my favorite lingerie set, a black satin-and-lace bra and panty ensemble with little pink bows on the front. I should have felt exposed and vulnerable standing there half naked while he was still fully dressed, but the way he looked at me, like I was something for him to devour, banished the thought.

He stepped closer, his hands finding my hips, then he turned me and guided me back until my thighs hit the mattress. One gentle push, and I was lying against the comforter.

He knelt on the floor between my legs, his hands sliding up my thighs, pushing them wider apart. When he hooked his fingers into my panties and pulled them down, I lifted my hips to help him. The cool air hit my heated skin, but then his mouth was on me and I stopped thinking altogether.

His tongue slid through my pussy in one slow stroke and I gasped, my back arching off the bed. He did it again, his hands gripping my thighs, holding me open for him. He took his time just as he'd promised, building the pleasure with maddening patience, giving me just enough to make me ache, but not enough to tip over.

My breasts felt full and sensitive, straining against my bra. I unhooked the clasp and let it fall to the floor. I fondled my own breasts, tweaked my nipples with my fingers, and moaned. At that moment, Liam seemed to decide he was done torturing me. He pushed two thick fingers deep inside and latched onto my clit. The combination made me cry out, my hips bucking against his mouth. He held me in place, his tongue working in quick circles while his fingers curved inside me, hitting exactly the right spot.

"Liam…" His name broke on a moan.

My hands found his hair, threading through it, my fingers tangling in the thick strands. I couldn't help the way my hips moved, couldn't stop the quivers rippling through my body or the way my legs fell open wider.

He groaned against me, the vibration sending me higher, and when he sucked harder, I shattered completely.

The orgasm ripped through me, stealing my breath, my vision going white at the edges. I heard myself cry out, loud and raw, but didn't care. His mouth stayed on me, drawing out the pleasure until I was shaking and trembling with aftershocks.

When the last tremor subsided, he finally lifted his head. His eyes met mine, dark and satisfied as he licked his lips. "Your pussy is like sweet honey, Morgan. I could feast on you all night."

As appealing as that sounded, I shook my head. "I need you inside of me. *Now.*"

He smirked at my impatience and stood, stripping off what remained of his clothes. Shoes, pants, his shirt, all landed in a pile on the floor. When he was finally naked, I couldn't look away. He was gorgeous. All lean muscle and tanned skin, his impressive cock hard and thick enough to make my core clench with anticipation. I bit my bottom lip, a low heat coiling inside me as I admired him. And there was a lot to admire.

"You like what you see?" he asked, ripping open a condom from his wallet and rolling it onto his cock with practiced ease.

"Yes," I breathed, even though I didn't think he really needed an answer. I was sure the look of awe on my face made it obvious that I liked it *very* much.

I moved backwards toward the pillows and Liam

joined me on the bed, fitting perfectly between my thighs. He kissed me, and I felt his erection slide along my slick pussy, the underside rubbing against my clit, more sensitive than usual because of my recent orgasm.

"Please, Liam," I begged as his lips trailed way too leisurely along my jaw and down my neck. "*Fuck me.*"

"Patience, Birthday Girl," he murmured huskily. "I'll get there. Promise."

His lips moved lower, his tongue tracing my collarbone, scattering kisses on my breasts. Then, he latched onto one of my nipples. An aching need took root as he sucked and licked, his hand teasing my other breast by lightly pinching my nipple. The sensations rocked through me, and I writhed impatiently beneath him, even though there was something intoxicating about the way he was making me wait.

He took his time lavishing one breast, then the other. His hot, hard, naked body felt so good against mine, and I ran my hands down his muscular back, enjoying the feel of him.

Finally, he moved back up and positioned the head of his cock at my entrance. "Look at me," he ordered softly.

I lifted my eyes to his and he pushed inside. The stretch was immediate and intense and I sucked in a startled breath. He was bigger than anyone I'd been with, and I shuddered at the way my body had to adjust to take him, how he filled me up in the most satisfying way.

"You okay?" His voice was strained, his arms braced on either side of me as he held my gaze.

I nodded, unable to speak, even as I appreciated his concern. Most men would have just kept going, only caring about chasing their own pleasure.

He started to move, slowly at first. Then, as I adjusted to him, his thrusts became harder, deeper. He was no longer gentle, and I didn't want him to be.

"So fucking tight," he murmured, lifting both of my legs onto his shoulders.

I was bent double, but the change in angle allowed him to go even deeper, the curve of his cock hitting that perfect spot inside me. I moaned, my hands reaching around and gripping his ass. There was something unbelievably erotic about the way his muscles clenched and released as he drove himself into me, over and over again.

I felt the beginnings of another orgasm gathering force inside me. "Liam…I'm almost there. I'm going to…"

"Do it," he rasped, keeping up the same relentless thrusts. "Come all over my cock, Morgan."

That commanding tone sent me spiraling. I broke apart beneath him, in the throes of passion and lost to the sublime ecstasy when I felt Liam's hips jerk hard. He buried himself deep and stilled, head thrown back, his guttural groan of pleasure erupting from him as he found his own release. The pulsing of his cock inside of me felt more intimate than I would have expected with a stranger I just met an hour ago.

He pressed his lips to mine, a soft kiss that chased the tremors still wracking my body. Warmth spread through my chest in a slow wave of feeling that had nothing to do with sex and everything to do with him.

"I'll be right back," he said, pulling out of me and heading into the bathroom.

A few minutes passed, and when he returned the condom was gone and he carried a warm, damp hand towel. He sat on the edge of the bed beside me, and instead of handing it to me, he gently cleaned me himself.

The gesture was so intimate it nearly undid me, considering no one had ever taken the time to do that for me before. My body was still humming from the pleasure he'd given me, and now this, his quiet care, the gentle sweep of warmth between my thighs…it made me feel stripped bare in a way I wasn't sure how to process.

"You okay?" he asked, as if sensing just how off-kilter I was feeling.

I nodded, not trusting my voice.

When he was done, Liam tossed the towel onto the bathroom floor, then came back, climbing into bed. The mattress dipped as he settled beside me, and he covered us both with the covers. Then he surprised me by gathering me close, so that I was snuggled up to his side. I hadn't expected that, or any of this extra tenderness or aftercare. For a moment, I wondered how a stranger's touch could feel so achingly right. Then he exhaled a slow, contented breath, and the answer didn't seem to matter.

I relaxed into his hold, thinking that this might just be the best birthday I'd ever had. For that matter, this man was the best lover I'd ever had. Dominant and considerate and hot as hell.

My eyelids grew heavy as I allowed myself to get comfortable. Just before I fell asleep, I felt Liam brush aside my hair and press a kiss to my forehead.

"Good night, Birthday Girl."

I smiled as I drifted off, content and happy with my decision to come here with him. But hours later, when I awoke to the sunrise coming through the big windows, I realized that I was alone. The other side of the bed was empty, the suite completely quiet.

A knot of disappointment twisted in my stomach as I pushed myself up, glancing around. He was definitely gone. There was no note. Nothing to even indicate that he'd been there, and the fact that he hadn't even bothered to at least say goodbye hurt more than it should have.

He hadn't made any promises. I knew that. This was supposed to be uncomplicated. A night of pleasure, and he'd certainly given me that. He'd been generous, attentive, and the sex had been mind-blowing. He'd ordered me cake, for God's sake.

Still, part of me had believed the softness in his voice, and the way he'd said, "Good Night, Birthday Girl", like our evening together meant something. Like maybe I had, too.

Clearly, I'd been mistaken. Again. What was wrong

with me that I always read more into situations with men than existed? That I believed that there was a connection when there was only the convenience of a hookup?

With a sigh, I lay back down and drew the covers tighter around me, trying to hold onto the fading warmth he'd left behind. But the truth settled in as quietly as the morning light filtering into the room.

Whatever last night had been, for him, it was already over. For me, I knew it was something I would never forget, along with a sharp reminder to stop confusing great sex with genuine connection.

CHAPTER FIVE

Liam

THE OCTOBER AIR was crisp as I made my way toward the tall glass building with Simon at my side. This New York City office building housed several businesses, but the one we were here to visit was GalvaTech, a small electronics company on the tenth floor.

As angel investors, Simon and I had been in negotiations with them for the past few months, and I was hopeful we were finally close to an agreement. I wanted to invest in the company. They weren't a big operation just yet, but I could see the potential for growth.

This was our first in-person meeting, though I'd already exchanged several emails and phone calls with the owner. Once we stepped out of the elevator on the tenth floor, we were faced with a glass door to the office of GalvaTech. Just inside the reception area, an older man with white hair and an easy smile waited for us.

"Welcome," he said, shaking both our hands with

undeniable enthusiasm. "I'm Samuel Starling."

The name matched the email correspondences. Samuel Starling was the founder and driving force behind GalvaTech. After a few quick pleasantries, he led us through the workspace beyond the lobby. The office was clean and efficient, lined with private offices and a large conference room enclosed with glass walls.

Employees bustled about, but none of them paid us any attention. Samuel led us straight to the conference room where a man was already seated at the long table, waiting for us. He stood when we entered and smoothed a hand down his tie.

"This is my stepson, Parker," Samuel said, introducing him. "He's our Chief Technology Officer."

After another round of handshakes and introductions, we all sat at the table. Simon and I were on one side, and Samuel and Parker sat on the other, right across from us. Parker had dark hair and grey eyes, and he looked tense, maybe even nervous, which I understood. Taking on an outside investor wasn't always an easy choice to make, but sometimes it was a necessary one to help the company reach its next stage of growth and ensure long-term success.

"I thought it was important that Parker be here," Samuel said, gesturing toward his stepson. "Since he designed the prototype for the new product that prompted your interest in GalvaTech, he's able to answer technical questions better than I can."

"Before we get to the actual product, why don't you tell us about your company," Simon said to

Samuel, taking out his iPad and jumping right to business. "We of course did research on our end, but we'd like to hear the specifics from you."

Samuel nodded and leaned back in his leather chair. "Well, I started GalvaTech about twenty years ago. Back then, we just made tantalum capacitors, which were used primarily in automotive systems and medical devices. After a while, we branched out into other electronic components. The company has grown slowly over the years from its modest beginnings, but I believe our new product has the potential to make the company more competitive on a global scale."

"Why don't you walk us through the particulars," I suggested, turning to Parker. I already had a pretty good understanding of what the device entailed, but I wanted his take as the inventor.

Parker shifted in his seat. "Well, what we've created is a new kind of portable electronic car charger. It's a level three, direct current, fast charger. That means it delivers power directly to the battery of an electric vehicle. This allows it to charge much faster than a level one or level two charger."

Simon typed a few notes onto his iPad. "And what makes your charger unique, besides speed?"

Parker grinned, his expression lighting up. "Our prototype is much smaller and more compact than others on the market. It can fit easily into the trunk of even a small EV. This allows for a level of convenience that hasn't been accomplished in the industry before."

There was pride in Parker's voice, and he had every right to feel that way. I agreed with his assessment. What he'd created was an amazing feat and the kind of innovation that could shift an entire market. But what impressed me the most was how intuitive this electronic car charger had the potential of being. It wasn't just another piece of tech. It solved a problem for those with electric cars who were reliant on charging stations. Parker made the solution look effortless.

I could already picture the rollout, the marketing angles, the potential partnerships, and the ripple effect it could have once consumers realized how much they needed the device. It was smart, scalable, and exactly the kind of product that could push GalvaTech to the next level.

And I wanted to be a part of that. I was excited enough about the portable charger and how it would impact the market to invest big money into this company.

"We have a functioning prototype," Samuel said, adding on to what Parker just said. "But we need capital for production and to create a strategy for a successful launch. We were thinking about five million."

My eyebrows lifted before I could stop them. That was a bold ask. For a company of GalvaTech's size, five million wasn't pocket change. It was a high-risk investment for a product that hadn't hit the market yet. Prototypes were one thing. Mass production and distribution was an entirely different beast.

Still, the fact that Samuel named that number without flinching said a lot. He wasn't throwing out a random figure. He genuinely believed the product could justify the funding. And as much as the investor in me wanted to push back, the strategist in me couldn't ignore the confidence behind his request.

Simon, however, wasn't as easily swayed. Not surprising, considering his more conservative approach to investments. He cleared his throat and folded his hands on the table, his expression thoughtful but firm. "At this time, we're prepared to invest three million," he said evenly. "We'll consider additional funding later, depending on performance. But you'll need to agree that Liam will oversee the product launch. He'll be present for the day-to-day operations for the time being, until that happens."

Parker frowned, and I didn't miss the tension flickering across his features. He clearly didn't like the proposed condition, but this would be nonnegotiable. With that much money on the line, Simon and I wanted someone onsite to ensure the launch went smoothly. We weren't just buying into a specific product, we were investing in a company and its future.

"That's really not necessary," Parker said stiffly. "We have a great team here. We can handle it."

"We're not criticizing your team in any way," I said, doing my best to placate him. "But GalvaTech's growth has been gradual until now. This launch is going to accelerate things quickly. If the operational stress is too high and isn't managed carefully, the company can become financially unstable and I can help make sure that doesn't happen.

"This condition is non-negotiable," Simon added, his tone leaving no room for argument.

A muscle ticked in Parker's jaw, but he gave a short nod, backing down.

"We agree to those terms," Samuel said, his tone brisk, as though he wanted to keep the meeting from derailing.

At the same time, Parker muttered under his breath, "She's not going to like this."

I opened my mouth to ask who *she* was, but the question died in my throat when a flicker of movement outside the conference room grabbed my attention. My focus shifted to the woman walking by and every muscle in my body tensed with shock as I took in the familiar, dark, silky brown hair. The strikingly poised and feminine profile. The same graceful stride I remembered from that night two weeks ago.

My heartbeat stumbled, then found a harder rhythm as I watched Morgan approach. She was wearing a dress, just like the night I met her, but this time it was conservative enough for the boardroom. No sexy cleavage on display, no glittery sash, no trace of the flirtatious woman I had met at the bar. Regardless, there was no disguising her killer hourglass figure.

I hadn't meant for that night with her to be anything more than a distraction, a few hours of sexy fun to silence the noise in my head after walking out of Noah's wedding reception. Instead, she'd gotten under my skin in ways that no woman had in years. For the past two weeks, she had randomly popped into my mind and I'd wondered what I had missed out on by leaving before she woke up. I'd even questioned if she and that night had been as mind-blowing as I remembered. Seeing her again, feeling that same visceral pull, I knew that it had been.

That night had been real. The chemistry, the conversation, all of it had been honest and unfiltered. The kind of connection that had the ability to sneak up on you and tear down walls you swore were impenetrable. She'd made me *feel* something again, and that unsettled me more than I wanted to admit.

I'd watched her sleep afterward, her expression soft, her hand resting against my chest like she belonged there, and that's when I panicked and freaked the fuck out.

I didn't do emotional entanglements anymore. Not after Ivy, who I'd given my trust and my damn heart, only to watch her walk away with someone else. Losing her hadn't just gutted me. It had convinced me that wanting anything deeper than temporary pleasure was a mistake I couldn't afford to make twice.

So, before morning came, I did what I'd taught myself to do best—I walked away. Before she could mean anything more.

But now, watching Morgan glide toward the conference room in that sleek black dress, my chest felt tight with something uncomfortably close to regret. I'd told myself ghosting her had been self-preservation. Looking at her now, I knew it hadn't been anything but cowardice.

She hadn't noticed me yet, even though she'd almost reached the doorway, and I braced myself for a reunion neither of us had ever expected.

CHAPTER SIX

Morgan

I WALKED INTO the conference room prepared to meet our potential new investors and came to an abrupt halt a few steps inside. Liam sat at the table with my father and stepbrother, staring right back at me with a look of clear surprise on his handsome face.

Shock rippled through me, knocking the air from my lungs. The sight of him brought that night back to me in a rush. The heat of his body. The intimacy that came after. And then, waking up alone in that hotel bed, humiliation twisting in my gut when I realized he'd ghosted me at some point during the night.

Since then, I'd told myself that it didn't matter, but that was a lie because I'd felt something real… and I'd let myself believe he had, too. It was a painful reminder that took me back to college, and to James. How I'd stupidly confused sex for something more.

Back then, the rejection had blindsided and crushed me. I thought I'd grown up, that I was smarter now, more careful, that I'd never let myself mistake chemistry for anything more ever again. Yet here I was, years later, realizing I'd made the same error in judgement with Liam. Only this time it cut deeper, because after years of protecting my heart and pushing men away, claiming I wanted fireworks, I'd let my guard down. For one reckless night, I'd allowed myself to feel something like hope.

Now I knew better. I'd been an easy lay for him, nothing more.

So, I straightened my shoulders, fixed my expression, and shored up my defenses because I was clearly going to need every ounce of composure I had to deal with the man I never thought I'd see again.

I'd known Parker and my father were meeting with potential investors today, hoping to hammer out the details of a contract, and I was late because of a call from HR that lasted longer than I'd anticipated. I wasn't just an employee of GalvaTech. It was my family's company. I owned shares in the business so this meeting was important to me as well.

Still, of all the investors in the city, of all the companies we could have partnered with, it was insane that the universe decided to throw Liam back into my life, this time on a professional level. It was equally unfair that he looked even more gorgeous now, wearing a tailored navy-blue suit that fit his body to perfection, and those eyes, still the same deep copper color I couldn't forget.

My father stood to greet me with a warm smile, jarring me back to the present. "Morgan, perfect timing," he said, sounding happy, which meant the meeting had gone well. "I was just about to call you in to meet our new investors."

I forced myself to move toward the conference table, to breathe and appear unaffected, to look anywhere but directly at Liam, even as my pulse hammered in my throat.

"Gentlemen, this is my daughter, Morgan. She's our marketing director," Dad said, a proud inflection in his voice. "Morgan, this is Liam and Simon Powers."

Both men stood, forcing me to glance their way. Keeping my expression neutral, I reached out to shake Simon's hand first. Then, because I had no choice, I turned to Liam and allowed him to slip his hand into mine. His fingers closed around my hand, warm and firm. The contact lasted a few seconds, but that spark of attraction I felt the night we met was still there. I pulled away quickly, refusing to meet his gaze.

"It's nice to meet you," I said curtly, making it clear with one sentence that we were going to act like we were strangers meeting for the first time. The last thing I wanted was anyone knowing I had slept with this man.

"Likewise," he said, the familiarity in his deep voice sending a shiver down my spine before I could stop it.

I shook off the sensation. It seemed that I'd come in on the tail end of the meeting because Dad was already discussing signing a contract once our lawyers looked it over. I didn't know all the details that had been worked out, but I'd find out later. Whatever terms they'd agreed on, there was no denying an influx of capital was needed and would help the company grow.

Parker walked up to me, a small frown furrowing his brows as he searched my expression. "Can I talk to you for a minute?" he asked me. "Privately?"

The request surprised me, but I nodded and followed my stepbrother out of the conference room. Once we were down the hallway and out of earshot, he stopped me with a hand on my arm and looked at me with concern in his eyes.

"What's wrong?" he asked.

"Nothing," I assured him.

Despite being stepsiblings, Parker and I had always been close. He was also perceptive, sometimes annoyingly so. I crossed my arms over my chest and did my best to project a nonchalance I didn't quite feel.

He studied me a moment before asking, "Do you know one of those men? Liam maybe?"

How had Parker even come to that conclusion? "Why would you ask that?"

He gave me a pointed look. "Because you looked like a deer in headlights when you walked into the conference room and saw him, not to mention how tense you were when you shook his hand. Neither of which is your normal confident way of handling yourself in a business setting."

"You're imagining things," I said, keeping my tone even. "I've never met Liam before today."

"Okay, I just wanted to make sure," Parker said, finally letting it go. "It's a good thing that you don't have a problem with him, because he's going to be working closely with us here in the office for the next few months. At least, that's how long I estimate it'll take to prepare the new product launch."

My stomach dipped. "What do you mean?" Investors were behind the scenes and periodically checked in. They didn't involve themselves in the business in any hands-on way.

"It's part of the contract terms," Parker said, grimacing as if the idea didn't appeal to him either. "They'll invest three million, but only if Liam oversees the launch and works with us day to day until everything is up and running. We're having our lawyers look over the contract, but barring any last-minute red flags, Samuel will be signing in the next few days, and Liam will be here in the office starting next week."

Anger flared through me at the new stipulation. "That's ridiculous. We know what we're doing. We don't need some outsider stepping in to supervise. This is our family's business, and we've managed just fine without anyone's oversight. It will change the entire dynamic of the office."

I tried to sound calm but my voice sharpened anyway. I wouldn't have been happy about this regardless, but the fact that it was Liam made dread twist in my stomach. I couldn't imagine working closely with him every single day.

"I agree," Parker said with a sigh as he rubbed a

hand along the back of his neck. "But if we want their money, which we do in order to get this portable charger to market, we don't have a choice."

We both looked back toward the conference room as my father, Liam, and Simon walked out together. Dad's enthusiasm filled the hallway, his voice carrying as he shook hands with the two men.

"This is exactly the kind of partnership GalvaTech needs," Samuel said, obviously excited at the prospect of working with them while Liam—God help me—smiled that same charming, persuasive smile I remembered all too well.

And all I could think was that he was going to be here. Every day. In my office. In meetings. In my space.

The thought made my stomach knot. I'd worked hard to build walls, to keep my life controlled and uncomplicated, and he had slipped past all of that far too easily. Pretending he meant nothing, that I didn't still feel that pull between us, was going to be its own kind of torture.

By the time Dad turned to me, still beaming, and said something about the exciting months ahead, I had my polite smile firmly back in place.

I didn't have a choice but to work with him, but I made myself a silent promise. I would never let Liam Powers catch me off guard again.

CHAPTER SEVEN

Liam

THE MOMENT MORGAN walked into that conference room I'd felt like someone had pulled the air right out of my lungs.

She froze when she saw me. Just for a second. But it was long enough to catch the shock of seeing me, then the flash of hurt in her eyes before she shoved it behind that perfectly composed expression. It was more than enough to remind me that ghosting her that night hadn't been my finest moment, and I'd been kicking myself for that decision ever since.

I attempted to keep my face neutral for the sake of everyone in the room, but the guilt hit me hard. We hadn't exchanged last names or phone numbers, and I hadn't expected to ever see her again, let alone at a company Simon and I were investing in that was her family's business. I couldn't decide if it was karma or fate that made our paths cross again in the most awkward way possible.

That night with Morgan—despite what she probably thought based on my actions—hadn't been something I'd brushed off like I had with every other woman since Ivy. Not even close. I left because staying scared the hell out of me. For the first time in years, I'd felt something I didn't know how to handle. But that reason didn't make my disappearing act any less insulting and I wasn't naïve enough to think my explanation for doing so would earn me any grace now.

Especially not in a conference room with her father and stepbrother watching us.

When I shook her hand, she kept her voice polite and distant. She pretended as though we'd never met before and I had followed suit, knowing if I'd pulled her aside in that moment—asked to speak with her or even hinted at recognition—everyone would have wondered why. There would be questions. Assumptions. Potential office gossip. And Morgan didn't deserve that. Not after the way I'd already mishandled things.

One thing I knew for certain was that I owed her an apology. I needed to fix the damage I'd done, if that was even possible. And I would, as soon as an opportunity presented itself.

So I'd stood there after our introduction, acting like a professional investor meeting a client for the first time, while my mind replayed the look in her eyes over and over. She'd probably spent the last two weeks convincing herself she'd meant nothing to me. That she'd misread everything that had transpired between us that night. That I was just another guy who took what he wanted and walked away.

And fuck, I'd let her think that. Christ, I felt like an asshole.

As the meeting ended and Samuel, Simon, and I headed out into the hallway where Parker and Morgan were discussing something, Morgan didn't so much as spare me another glance. And that, more than anything, told me exactly how deeply my actions had affected her.

Starting next week, I'd be in this office. Every day. Working beside her. Seeing her in meetings, hearing her voice, and watching her act as though we were strangers. But we weren't. Not even close.

We parted ways with Samuel, and Simon and I made our way to the elevator. Once inside, Simon pressed the button for the lobby and glanced at me.

"Let's go catch an early dinner to celebrate," he suggested.

"Like we haven't spent enough money today already?" I asked, forcing myself to grin so Simon didn't suspect that anything was wrong.

Simon snorted. "Please. The day I pass up an excuse to eat a good meal is the day I no longer have a pulse." His mouth curved into a self-satisfied smile. "We closed a good deal and I'm celebrating whether you come with me or not. I was thinking Italian. There's a place not far from here that I want to try."

Simon made the decision without asking my opinion, which was typical of his detail-obsessed personality, but I didn't care, especially not today. My mind was too preoccupied with thoughts of Morgan. As we taxied to the restaurant, Simon kept talking about timelines, projections, and product specs, but it all washed over me in pieces. Every word reminded me that in a few days I would be working alongside the woman I hadn't been able to forget, and that I'd already screwed up any possibility of a second chance with.

The restaurant Simon picked was an upscale establishment with the smell of garlic and tomatoes thick in the air. Once we'd settled at the table and ordered an expensive bottle of red wine, Simon leveled me with a serious look.

"What's going on with you?" he asked, clearly noticing how distracted I'd been. "Is there an issue with the investment deal that I'm not seeing?"

Of course he'd think my quiet mood was business related. "No." I shook my head and quickly reassured him. "The deal's fine."

"Then what is it?" he persisted, swirling the red liquid in his wine glass. "Because you've been off since the second half of our meeting with Samuel, and definitely pre-occupied since we left GalvaTech."

My stomach knotted and I exhaled a deep breath, knowing I needed to come clean with Simon. "I just…wasn't expecting to see someone I knew at the office."

Simon blinked at me in surprise. "Who?"

"Morgan. Samuel's daughter."

His brows raised in surprise. "And how do you

know her? Because the two of you didn't exactly seem friendly when Samuel introduced her to us."

I hesitated. Simon was my business partner, but he was also my brother and one of my best friends. And he had a sixth sense for when I was holding something back. I didn't want to lie to him about the details of how I knew Morgan.

"We met a few weeks ago," I said carefully. "At a bar."

It didn't take long for understanding to dawn on his face. "The night of Noah's wedding."

I nodded, my fingers tightening on the stem of my wine glass.

"And you didn't think to mention the fact that you hooked up with Samuel's daughter before we signed a three-million-dollar deal with her family's company?"

"I didn't know she worked there. I didn't know her last name." I ran a hand through my hair, my own frustration getting the best of me. "We didn't exactly exchange a lot of personal information."

Simon swore beneath his breath. "Please tell me you didn't do your usual fuck 'em and leave 'em routine—"

"Yeah, I did." I opted for honesty and full disclosure, as painful as it was to admit. "Even worse, I ghosted her without an explanation. While she was sleeping."

"Jesus, Liam." Simon sat back in his seat, staring at me with blatant disbelief. "Of all the women you could have fucked, literally and figuratively, it had to be the daughter of the man we're now in business with?"

I grimaced, because yeah, when he put it that way it sounded even worse than it already was between Morgan and me.

Thankfully, the waitress arrived with our orders, setting our plates of pasta in front of us. Simon took a few bites of his carbonara before returning to our conversation, which I'd been hoping he'd drop.

"Are you going to be able to handle working with her every day? Because if this is going to be a problem—"

"It won't be." I met his gaze from across the table. "I'll handle it."

Simon let out a dry laugh. "Handling it means more than ignoring the situation, Liam. You need to actually fix what you fucked up."

"I know," I said, my tone defensive.

"No, I don't think you do." He pointed his fork at me. "Because if you did, you'd be sweating bullets right now. This isn't some random woman you'll never see again. This is Morgan Starling. She works there. Her father owns the damn place. And we just tied three million dollars to their company."

That was Simon. Telling it like it was. No filtering or softening his words. Not that he was wrong.

"I get it," I muttered, pushing my lasagna around on my plate.

"Do you?" Simon cocked his head. "Because I'm not sure you've fully grasped how royally you've screwed yourself. And me. And possibly this deal if she decides to make your night together an issue. Christ, Liam, you need to fix this yesterday."

I let out a rough exhale, fighting the urge to snap back. "I *said* I'll talk to her."

"No," he said firmly. "Not talk. Fucking grovel."

I scrubbed a hand over my tense jaw. "Groveling seems…overly dramatic."

"Dramatic is ghosting a woman who obviously caught your attention enough to want to fuck then showing up in her conference room like an unexpected plot twist no one saw coming," Simon shot back, not mincing words. "Groveling is bare-minimum damage control."

I dropped my silverware onto my plate with a clatter, my irritation flaring hotter than I intended. "What do you want me to say? 'Sorry I panicked and had a minor emotional meltdown after having the best night I've had in years with a woman'?"

"Honestly?" Simon dared to smirk. "That's not a terrible start."

I glared at him.

He held up a hand. "Look, I'm not trying to bust your balls more than necessary, though let's be real, you deserve some degree of ball-busting here." He took a sip of wine, then fixed me with a level look. "But if you don't want this to blow up in our faces, you need to make things right with her."

"I plan to."

"Well, you're not exactly Mr. Emotional Availability these days," Simon said, pointing out my flaws in a way that only a brother could. "So what do you have in mind?"

"I'll apologize," I said. "A real apology. Not some bullshit excuse."

"Good," Simon said with an approving nod. "And sooner rather than later, before she convinces HR that you're a walking liability."

I huffed out a humorless laugh and drained the last of the wine in my glass, wishing it was something much stronger.

From across the table, Simon studied me intuitively. "Do you…like her? I mean, beyond the sex, is there something else there?"

I didn't answer right away when I should have replied with a swift *no*. How could I explain that Morgan had gotten under my skin in a way no one had since Ivy? That leaving her that night had been about protecting myself, not dismissing her and what we'd shared.

When I didn't respond, Simon's expression softened, but his voice remained firm. "Look, whatever this thing is between you two? Deal with it. Apologize. Clear the air. Because if you go into that office next week with all that negative energy unresolved, you're both going to be miserable."

"And the investment deal?" I asked, wanting to make sure Simon wasn't worried about my personal mess bleeding into our professional one.

"The deal will survive," he said confidently. "As long as you don't act like a complete idiot twice."

"Thanks for the vote of confidence."

"Anytime." He twirled his fork in his pasta. "Now eat before I take your plate and finish your lasagna for you. You're clearly too stressed to appreciate a good meal."

He wasn't wrong about that. I picked up my fork, but my appetite was gone. All I could think about was Morgan and how much I'd earned every bit of her disappointment. And how badly I needed to make things right between us.

"So, since you're going to be spending most of your time at GalvaTech for the foreseeable future," Simon said, wiping his mouth with his napkin, "I'd like to borrow your assistant to help me go over the financial reports and performance metrics for Stark, Inc. If we decide to invest in that business, I want to know everything about them and I need someone competent to run those stats."

It took me a moment to realize what he was asking. "Wait a minute, why would you need to borrow Clara for that when you have your own assistant?"

Simon shrugged. "Lisa wasn't working out so I had to let her go."

I gaped at him in disbelief. "You fired *another* assistant? That's the fourth one this year. What the hell is going on with you?"

He didn't even flinch, just casually refilled his wineglass. "What can I say. I have high expectations."

That was putting things mildly when it came to Simon's rigid personality. "And what did this one do to earn your disdain?"

"She forgot to pick up my dry cleaning *and* she used the wrong version of *there* in a company-wide memo. It was supposed to be t-h-e-r-e. Not t-h-e-i-r."

I stared at him incredulously. "Seriously? You fired her over those two small grievances? Those are minor issues, and she only worked for you for a couple of weeks."

"Forgetfulness and lack of attention to detail are issues that can snowball into a full-blown crises," he said matter-of-factly. "I don't have the time to double check every email and document because I can't trust the person doing the work. I need an assistant that I can rely on to not make crucial mistakes."

He said it with his typical no-nonsense certainty, but I could see the tightness around his mouth and knew exactly what he was referring to.

Last year, his assistant Olivia had screwed up badly. Missed a key deadline, misfiled critical documents, and cost us a major deal that made us look like amateurs in the industry, which we were not. Simon had never forgiven her…or himself. He'd taken the mistake personally, like her failure reflected directly on his abilities as a leader, and he'd never really gotten over that hit to his pride.

"Simon…" I exhaled, letting my tone soften just a fraction. "You need to let that go."

He didn't look at me or respond, choosing instead to focus his attention on adjusting the silverware on the table.

"Fine," I said with a sigh, giving in. "I'll tell Clara to help you out, but if your grumpy ass scares her off, I'll be furious."

Simon rolled his eyes and grunted, which I took to mean that he agreed to behave.

We finished our meal, or at least Simon devoured the rest of his pasta, and we parted ways, both of us heading home. It had been a long day and by the time I walked into my high-rise apartment, exhaustion dragged at me.

I settled on the couch, let my head fall back against the cushion and released a long breath, feeling as though everything in my life was about to change. My close proximity to Morgan was inevitable, and whether it complicated my life or not, I was ready to face the tension between us head on, instead of avoiding it.

Because the more I tried to deny the truth of what I had felt that night, the more some part of me pushed back. I was running out of ways to pretend those feelings for Morgan didn't exist or matter.

However, what I should or would do about that realization was something I'd yet to figure out.

CHAPTER EIGHT

Morgan

I WAS AN early riser, which meant that I was one of the first to arrive at the office Monday morning. I liked the quiet before the chaos. It gave me time to settle in, go over my schedule, and organize everything that I needed for business meetings throughout the day.

As I stepped off the elevator, my mind was fully focused on work, until I saw that I wasn't the first one here. As I headed to my office, I walked past the one right next to mine that had been empty for over a year.

The light was on, and I could hear someone moving around inside. Pausing in the doorway, I peeked inside and saw that it was Liam, setting up shop right next to where I worked every day.

He was moving the desk closer to the wall opposite the door. His suit jacket had been discarded, and his shirt sleeves were rolled up. His muscular forearms made my mouth water, as did the flex of his ass muscles while he shoved the large, heavy desk into place.

Of course he looked sexy and attractive at seven in the morning. And of course my body betrayed me before my brain could catch up. My stomach dipped, my chest tightened, and a rush of warmth spread through me so fast it threw me off kilter.

I replaced that traitorous attraction with annoyance. I knew he'd be based here at the office for the next few months, but I wasn't expecting to see him so early his first day on the job. Having to deal with Liam as my first interaction of the morning didn't thrill me, especially since we were the only ones here.

I lingered a moment too long, and Liam must have sensed my presence. He turned around and caught me watching him.

"Uh…hi," I said, hating the breathless quality of my voice. Heat crept up my neck, because he'd definitely noticed me staring. "I didn't expect to see you here."

"I like to get an early start when it's quiet," he said, offering me a smile even as his gaze took in the outfit I'd worn today—tailored black slacks and a pink silk blouse with heels. "It gives me time to get my to-do list organized before the day begins."

I hated that I understood what he meant. The last thing I wanted was to find some kind of common ground with him. He was *supposed* to be nothing more than a professional obligation until the product launch, nothing more.

I cleared my throat and pointed vaguely behind me. "Well, my office is right next door." I wasn't sure why I even told him that. It came out sounding like an invitation, and that annoyed me even more.

"Morgan…I didn't know you worked here," he suddenly said before I could turn around and walk away, his gaze steady on mine. "When we negotiated the terms of the contract with your father, which was by email and phone, I had no idea you were a part of the company."

We were getting dangerously close to discussing the night we'd spent together, but I had no desire to hash out our personal history. It was much safer to pretend it never happened, for the sake of working together and for my pride.

"I get that," I replied, keeping my tone cool, dismissive even. "We're just strangers, after all."

His jaw flexed, a tiny tic that told me the words hit something he didn't like. "Morgan, about that night," he said quietly, the rough edge of sincerity in his voice catching me off guard. "I shouldn't have left the way I did."

The apology landed like a weight in the center of my chest, making my heart squeeze tight. He looked and sounded like he regretted his actions, but my own self-preservation had me shrugging indifferently. "It's fine. Really."

His brows pulled together. "Leaving you without at least saying goodbye wasn't *fine*," he said firmly. "I want you to know that the attraction and connection between us was real, and I'm sorry for the way I left things between us. The issue was me, not you, and you deserved better than waking up alone…and me being gone."

I suspected there was more to his reason for bolting in the middle of the night, and it was possibly tied into the story he'd told me about his ex-fiancée leaving him just weeks before their wedding. I could only assume he had his guard up when it came to women, which was something I could relate to after my situation with James. Still, I wasn't about to make the mistake of softening toward him on a personal level again, knowing he had commitment issues.

I just wish my damn body would get that memo.

"Liam, we're adults and it was a one night thing," I said, keeping my tone nonchalant, like our time together had been nothing more than a forgettable blip on my radar, even though I still felt that strong attraction to him even now. "No expectations, no follow-up from you required. You don't owe me anything because it certainly didn't mean anything more than just sex to me," I lied.

Frustration flickered across his face at my dismissive attitude. "I still should have handled the situation better."

"Okay," I said, because what else was there to say? "Apology accepted."

His frown deepened as he walked a bit closer. "I'm serious, Morgan."

I took equal steps back, needing to maintain that distance between us. "And I heard you. We're good. Really. It's not worth thinking about."

He stopped and studied me in a way that made my skin heat. "Is that really what you believe?" he asked after a few silent beats, his voice dropping lower. "That it didn't mean anything other than just sex?"

My heart stammered, but I forced myself to hold his gaze. "What else would I think?"

His jaw worked, and for a second I thought he might argue, or give me something to indicate that maybe he'd felt more that night, too. Which was stupid, wishful thinking on my part, especially when he finally replied.

"I just want us to be okay," he said, running a hand through his thick hair. "Working together, I mean. I don't want things to be…tense or awkward between us."

And there it was. The real reason for this conversation and his apology. It was all business. Professional courtesy. Damage control.

Something cold settled in my chest, but I didn't let it show. "Right," I said, nodding as if that made perfect sense. "Of course. If that's what you're worried about, you can relax. There's no reason why we can't keep things professional in the office."

He looked at me again, searching my face like he was trying to find something more. Whatever he was looking for, I wasn't going to give it to him and kept my expression schooled.

"Good," he said quietly, though his frown didn't fade. "That's…good."

The silence stretched between us, and I broke it

first. "I should get to work."

"Wait," he said, just as I started toward my office.

I stopped, and for a moment my pulse leapt as I waited for him to speak.

"So…I'm ordering lunch for the whole office today," he said, jarring me with the segue into professional small talk. "It's something I always do for a new company that I'm working with. What would you like?"

Of all the things I thought he might say, lunch hadn't even been on the list. I blinked at him, regrouped, and latched onto the safest answer possible. "If you want to appeal to everyone, you should probably go with pizza."

Liam tilted his head to the side as he leaned against the front of his desk and folded his arms across his chest. "I asked what *you* would like," he said, smiling in that charming way of his. "What's *your* favorite food?"

I swallowed hard, trying my hardest not to let my attraction to him get the better of me. "Sushi. I'm nuts about the stuff. There's a place about two blocks away where I go for lunch all the time. But for the office employees, you should stick with pizza."

He gave a nod. "Okay, pizza it is."

His eyes met mine, and the air between us tightened. I felt the awareness instantly, low in my stomach, warm and unwelcome. His gaze dipped to my mouth for the briefest second, just long enough to make me remember his hot, deep kisses, before flicking back up to my eyes.

My pulse stumbled and I straightened, needing to do something that made me feel like I was back in control again. "Well, I'm sure you have things to do before everyone gets into the office. Have a good day, Mr. Powers."

"You too, Ms. Starling," he drawled, his low, deep voice doing annoyingly intimate things to my body.

I turned quickly, refusing to glance back as I made my way to my own office right next to his. I shut the door behind me, leaned against it, and had to press a hand to my chest to steady both my heart rate and my breathing.

I needed distance. I needed focus. I needed Liam Powers out of my head. Because after ten minutes alone with him this morning, I already knew one thing with absolute, undeniable certainty. Working in the same office as Liam was going to be a problem. A very sexy, complicated, distracting problem.

Because no matter how hard I tried to pretend otherwise, no matter his genuine apology or our resolve to keep things professional, it was clear that at least on my part, the attraction and chemistry between us hadn't abated one bit.

CHAPTER NINE

Liam

MY FIRST WEEK at GalvaTech was busy, which was to be expected when starting with a new company. As usual, I spent my first day setting up my office and introducing myself to everyone, buying lunch and giving the employees a chance to get to know me and establishing a comfortable working dynamic. Now that I'd been here almost a week, I had a routine in place.

When I started the angel investment company with Simon after leaving Wall Street, I discovered early on that coming into an already established company was a delicate process. Feathers were easily ruffled when a new guy showed up and started throwing his weight around. It didn't matter if my experience in business made my ideas valuable. It didn't even matter that I invested a significant amount of money into the business.

People were touchy about strangers bossing them around, so I learned that it was best to spend a few days observing how things ran and working closely with the CEO to make it clear that this was a collaborative effort and that I wasn't just some rich asshole coming in to take over. This was a partnership, not a takeover.

Most everyone seemed more relaxed around me now. While learning how things operated and were managed across the company, I was particularly impressed with how Samuel ran things at GalvaTech. He was hands-on without being overbearing. He checked in with each department regularly but also trusted his executives and managers to run things as needed. He delegated responsibilities in a way that made people feel supported instead of micromanaged.

He was a down-to-earth guy that cared about his company in a way that only a man that built it from the ground up could. It was clear to me that the success of this company meant the world to him because it was his legacy, and that feeling was reflected among his children.

His stepson, Parker, was vital to the company. I quickly realized that he didn't just design the new product. He oversaw the research and development department and managed technology infrastructure. By all accounts, the man was a computer genius.

Morgan was the marketing director for the company, and even just a cursory review of her department told me that she was damn good at her job. She'd taken GalvaTech from a mid-level name to a recognizable brand in a few short years. She had a passion for this work that was obvious without even having to talk to her.

Which was convenient, considering how she'd avoided me completely.

After our awkward conversation when I was setting up my new office, I knew that keeping things professional with her wasn't going to be nearly as easy as she made it sound that morning. She talked about our night together as if it didn't matter, and I figured I had that coming for sneaking out, but I also knew it was best to put it behind us so that my investment and her family's company could be our focus.

But telling myself that and actually doing it? Two very different things.

I couldn't seem to *stop* thinking about the night we slept together, and it was all because of her. Morgan was too damn tempting in her pencil skirts and high heels that did amazing things for her ass.

Not that I was staring at it. Nope, not at all. Especially not when I was in a meeting with her father and she walked by the conference room. That would be incredibly unprofessional.

I also didn't get turned on by the deep red lipstick she was wearing today or fantasize about that mouth wrapped around my dick. My hands didn't itch to be buried in her silky brown hair and I *definitely* didn't long to spread her out on my desk and bury my face between her legs again just to hear her moan my name.

Because I was businessman, entirely focused on the job I was here to do.

"Liam, did you hear me?" Samuel asked.

I internally cringed as I realized all those dirty thoughts that I *wasn't* having about Morgan had completely distracted me while I was supposed to be speaking with Samuel about the strategy going forward.

After almost a week of observing and getting to know everyone, it was time to develop and execute a plan to achieve goals related to the mobile EV charger. At least, that was what I put in the memo when I arranged this meeting with Samuel. So far, the conversation hadn't gotten far because my eyes tracked Morgan's stroll from her office to the elevator a moment ago.

Feeling guilty checking out the woman in front of her father—as much as I tried to convince myself that wasn't what I was doing—I cleared my throat and refocused my attention on Samuel. He looked at me with nothing but patience in his expression, and I figured he must not have realized exactly what had diverted my focus.

That was fortunate.

"I'm sorry," I said, straightening the papers on the table in front of me just to give myself something to do with my hands. "My mind wandered for a moment. What did you say?"

"I was saying that I think the best way to move forward is to team you up with a member of my staff that will work directly with you to make sure the launch of the EV charger goes well. Someone that is familiar enough with all aspects of the business to be a liaison between you and the other employees."

That made sense. "Who do you have in mind?"

Samuel smiled. "Morgan would be the best person for the job. I know you haven't had a chance to interact with her much since you started at the office, but she doesn't just hold her position as the marketing director because she's my daughter. She's great at her job, and I know she'll have plenty of innovative ideas to offer for launching the product."

"If you think that's best," I said, carefully keeping my expression blank.

Morgan is going to hate this.

And me? Well, working that closely with her every day was going to wreck my focus, because if there was one thing I realized over the past few days, it was that my attraction to Morgan hadn't faded one damn bit. Sharing space with her, breathing in her scent and noticing every small detail about her was going to blur lines I was already struggling to keep straight.

"Great," Samuel said with a grin as he cuffed me on the shoulder. "I'll let her know so that you can get started right away. Should I have her come to your office this afternoon?"

"Sure. We can meet after lunch."

The rest of the morning passed quickly, and I spent most of my time reviewing market analysis reports about mobile EV chargers. I left for an hour during lunch, meeting Simon at a cafe about halfway between our firm and GalvaTech, where we went over the details of the new company that he was looking into for us to potentially invest in. My assistant had been helping him with that research for the past few days, but I knew by the texts I'd received from Clara that she was getting tired of his bossy attitude. I gave Simon a week to hire his own assistant before I contacted a temp agency.

When I returned to the office, I'd barely settled into my chair when there was a brisk knock at the door.

"Come in," I called out.

Morgan stepped inside and shut the door behind her. She didn't bother hiding how unenthused she was about being assigned by her father to work directly with me. Still, she managed to look composed and professional, and I still felt that damn spark of awareness between us.

"Hello, Morgan," I said, gesturing to one of the two chairs in front of my desk. I had a more comfortable sitting area in the corner of the room—a small black leather couch and matching armchair—but I figured it was better to keep things formal. "Thanks for joining me."

"I'm not sure there was much of a choice," she said, keeping her tone carefully neutral. "Dad said that he wants us to work together on this product launch."

I tipped my head, not missing the flicker of resistance in her eyes. "And you have a problem with that?"

She sighed as she sank into the chair in front of me. "Of course not. Why would I?"

She was a terrible liar, and I actually liked that about her. The way her honesty slipped through the cracks even when she was trying to play it cool. "I guess we should get started then."

Morgan had a tablet in her hand, and she turned her attention to the device. "Great. I have a lot of ideas, but I'm wondering about your timeline. When do you envision this product launch taking place?"

I paused, staring at her a moment as I took in the change she made when we shifted to business. Her agitation disappeared, and the crease in her forehead flattened out. Maybe we'd be able to work together without too much trouble after all.

"I was thinking six months," I said.

"So, early May?" She swiped open a calendar on her tablet with quick, efficient movements.

"Let's make it the first of May," I suggested. "Start the month out right. That way, we should see the results in the second quarter's financial reports."

I watched her make a note of the launch date on her tablet. I stood up and walked around my desk. My office was large, and I'd pushed the desk to the wall for a reason. I liked to move around while I was thinking. The space between the desk and the entrance was perfect for pacing.

Morgan watched me curiously as I tracked the length of the office, tossing a red stress ball from one hand to the other while I spoke.

"Since the prototype's already been tested and approved, we're starting ahead of the curve on manufacturing. The funds we're investing can go straight toward mass production."

"Parker can take care of that," Morgan said, turning her chair so she could face me as I walked back and forth. She crossed one leg over the other, and for a second I forgot my next thought entirely.

I glanced out the window at the city skyline, anchoring myself back to the conversation. "He told me the same thing. That's convenient, and it frees us up to focus on the ultimate goal. Making sure this thing sells."

I turned around to find Morgan smiling. "I'm way ahead of you there." She swiped through her screen on her tablet, then stood up to show me a chart.

"I researched industry trends over the last couple of days, and I created this graph of how I expect the launch to go if we take advantage of three key points," she said enthusiastically. "First, the high demand for faster charging capabilities. Second, the projected growth of electric vehicle charging stations, which is expected to expand exponentially over the next five years. Finally, we need to take into account the competition between North America and Europe to get ahead in this industry. We might be leading the technology here, but there are a few companies that are working on similar products overseas."

"Wow," I said, blown away by her strategic thinking and in-depth grasp of the industry in general. I stopped pacing completely and she had my full attention. "I'm impressed."

She narrowed her eyes at me, like she couldn't decide if that was flattery or an insult. "You sound surprised."

"Sorry." This time, I couldn't keep myself from grinning. "That was definitely meant as a compliment."

"Part of my job is conducting market research to identify ideal customers and create strategies to reach them," she said, her tone cool and pointed. "I didn't get this job because of nepotism. I *earned* it."

Her father had said as much to me this morning but hearing her defend herself so fiercely was surprisingly endearing. There was pride in the set of her shoulders and the stubborn tilt of her chin, and I felt a startling rush of affection for her. I nearly acted on it, my hand starting to reach out to cup her cheek before I caught myself and shoved my fingers through my hair the way I always did when I was frustrated.

Usually, that reaction was somehow related to work but this time, it was all tangled up with Morgan and the desire she stirred in me without even trying. I wasn't used to that.

"Here," she said, angling the tablet toward me. "Take a look at the report."

I stepped in closer and looked at the chart she'd created. Even just a quick glance told me that she'd accurately applied the information she'd researched to create a reasonable expectation of profitability within the first three months of launching the EV charger.

I didn't say anything for a moment, and she bit her

bottom lip as she looked at me expectantly, watching my reaction to the chart. The way she worried her bottom lip—soft, deliberate, unguarded—knocked the air out of my lungs. And suddenly, I wasn't thinking about market projections anymore. I was thinking about her mouth. And kissing her.

Shit.

Her scent permeated my senses, wreaking havoc with my good intentions. This was the part I hadn't prepared for, the effect she had on me that only grew stronger the closer we stood. I had convinced myself I could handle working beside her, but I'd clearly underestimated how damn tempting she would be. The pull I felt toward her was barely controllable.

Or maybe it wasn't controllable at all, because before I could think better of it, my hand lifted and I found myself tucking a loose strand of hair behind her ear, then running the pad of my thumb over her cheek.

Morgan froze, seemingly startled by my spontaneous touch. Her eyes widened a fraction, her breath catching as her lashes fluttered. Color crept into her cheeks and she swallowed hard, her gaze locked on mine. She wasn't leaning in, but she wasn't backing away either, and that tiny bit of permission felt like a match dropped on gasoline.

The air thickened between us, charged enough to make my pulse thrum through my veins. My whole body tightened with the urge to close the last few inches and taste her again.

But I had something I needed to say first. Something that mattered more than impulse.

"I never doubted your intelligence or your work ethic," I said in response to her comment about nepotism. "I already knew you earned your place here."

Her features shifted in an instant, her eyes softening, and her lips parting, just slightly. Her open, unreserved expression hit me so hard it felt like the ground shifted beneath us. Shockingly, she tilted her face up to mine, the invitation subtle, but unmistakable.

An undeniable hunger for her took hold and I lowered my head, not a single rational thought left in my body. Her breath mingled with mine, our lips close enough that I could feel the whisper of her exhale.

Just before we kissed, there was a knock on the office door.

CHAPTER TEN

Morgan

I JOLTED AT the sound of a knock. My heart was racing, and my core clenched with arousal, but I suddenly felt like I had been doused with ice water as Liam stepped away. He rounded his desk to put distance between us as he called out for whoever was interrupting us to enter.

I had no chance to pull myself together before the door opened, and I was sure that I looked rattled by the almost kiss that I so desperately, foolishly wanted. My cheeks felt warm, so I was probably flushed, and my breathing was unsteady.

So, I wasn't thrilled when it was Parker that walked into the office. It just *had* to be someone that knew me well enough to notice that I wasn't my normal calm and composed self.

Thankfully, he didn't spare me more than a passing glance. His focus went to Liam as he stepped behind one of the chairs in front of the desk, gripping the backrest with tight, white-knuckled fingers.

I knew Parker just as well as he knew me, so it only

took one glance at him to know he was having a bad day physically. His shoulders were tense, and there was sweat glistening on his brow. His jaw was tight, and he was taking slow, deliberate breaths in through his nose and out of his mouth.

I recognized those signs. He was in pain.

"Are you okay?" I asked, the heat of sexual tension with Liam shoved instantly aside. "Is it your back?"

"Yeah," he grunted. "I guess I slept in the wrong position last night."

Liam looked between the two of us, confusion creasing his brow.

"Parker hurt his back about four years ago," I explained. "He had a herniated disc and had to have back surgery."

"I'm mostly fine, but I still get a little stiff sometimes," Parker explained, one of his hands going to his lower back and rubbing in a tight circle. "Sorry for the interruption, but Dad sent me."

"What does he need?" Liam asked, accepting the subject change easily.

"He'd like to speak with you if you have time."

Liam's gaze shifted to me, and I shrugged. "Go ahead. We can finish our marketing conversation later." I needed a little distance after that near kiss anyway.

"Okay," Liam said, his eyes dropping briefly to my lips before he looked away. "I'll go talk to him now."

He left the office without another word, and I had to wonder if he was as flustered as I was by what almost happened between us. As soon as he was gone, I let out a breath I didn't realize I was holding.

"What's going on?" Parker asked once we were alone.

"I don't know what you mean." I ducked my head, pretending I needed to check the calendar on my tablet.

"Don't be obtuse, Morgan," Parker said, gesturing to the door that Liam just exited through, then winced because the jerky movement caused him pain. "You're seriously going to pretend I didn't walk in on a moment?"

I tried to maintain a poker face. "You're clearly imagining things."

"And you're a bad liar," he countered. "You both looked guilty when I walked in here, and you were blushing."

"You're too observant for your own good," I muttered beneath my breath.

I wasn't going to admit to anything going on between us, but I also felt my cheeks growing warm once again as I remembered the way Liam almost kissed me. And how much I'd wanted it.

"You're blushing again," Parker pointed out.

I sighed.

"Listen, I'm not trying to give you a hard time, and you *know* I've never been one to interfere in your love life, but you and Liam…that's a bad idea." His lips pursed with disapproval. "The two of you hooking up wouldn't be good for business."

His words landed hard because I already knew Parker was right. Hearing him say it out loud just made the truth impossible to ignore. I was playing with fire. And for what? A man who had disappeared the first time I'd slept with him? A man who made it very clear he was emotionally unavailable?

The attraction wasn't worth the risk. Not to the job, and certainly not to my pride.

Of course, it was easier to be resolute about the situation when Liam wasn't standing three inches away, looking at me like he wanted to ruin my self-control all over again.

"Don't worry," I said. "There's nothing going on between us."

There was a moment of tense silence as Parker studied me. Finally, he gave a curt nod.

"Okay, I'll let it go," he said, his brows still furrowed. "I just…I don't want anything to compromise our business arrangement with Liam."

"Me neither," I assured him. I didn't want to linger on this conversation, so I pivoted fast. "How's Becca doing? It's been a while since I've talked to her."

Parker grinned. It was a little strained because of his lingering back pain, but I knew he was trying his best to act normal. "She's good. Still dealing with some heartburn, but she had it with the first pregnancy too. It's manageable."

I laughed. "She'd probably disagree." I remember her complaining about those symptoms when she was pregnant with Gracie four years ago.

"Yeah, probably," he admitted, rubbing at his back again. "Actually, that reminds me. Would you mind babysitting tomorrow night? It's been a while since I took Becca out, and I wanted to treat her to a nice dinner."

"Of course," I said immediately, since I had no set plans for Friday evening. "I love spending time with Gracie."

We parted ways and I walked back to my own office, closed the door, and set my tablet down, determined to actually focus on work this time. No more replaying almost-kisses, heated looks, or imaginary scenarios where Liam Powers forgot what professional boundaries were.

Time to get my head on straight and keep it that way. For real.

"I GOTS THE nail polish," Gracie said, walking into the kitchen with her little hands full of the colorful glass bottles.

I'd just finished loading our dinner plates into the dishwasher, so I rushed over and rescued the glass containers before they tumbled to the floor and made a mess. Gracie followed me to the kitchen table. I'd been babysitting for about an hour. We started off with a game of hide and seek before eating a simple dinner of spaghetti and green beans, the three-year-old's current favorite meal.

Now, I assumed she wanted pretty fingernails. "So, we're giving each other manicures, huh?"

Gracie shook her head. "No, I gonna paint *your* nails," she said, correcting my assumption.

"Well," I said, fighting a laugh. "I guess I'm the client tonight."

I grabbed the nail polish remover from the bathroom to remove the red color I was already wearing. This was going to be a huge mess, but honestly, I didn't care. There was no universe in which I'd tell my adorable niece no.

She insisted on doing each nail a different color, and I ended up with more polish on my skin than my nails. But half an hour later, we were done, and she looked so proud of her work that I made sure to make a big fuss over how much I loved it.

Once the nail polish was dry, we went into the living room and turned on a Disney movie. I grew up watching the classics, but Gracie's current favorite was about a Scottish girl with a bow and arrow that accidentally turned her mom into a bear. I actually enjoyed it and got so wrapped up in watching the movie that I didn't immediately notice when Gracie fell asleep on the couch beside me.

When her little snores reached my ears, I looked over to see her sprawled out on her back, her long eyelashes resting against her cheek and her dark curls haloed around her head. She looked so cute that my heart swelled with affection.

Carefully lifting her into my arms, I carried her up

the stairs to her bedroom and settled her onto her toddler mattress. She'd already changed into pajamas right after dinner, so all I had to do was tuck the covers around her and turn on her nightlight before slipping out of the room.

I'd just pulled the door closed behind me when my phone started to ring in my pocket. I flinched at the sudden sound before rushing down the hall away from Gracie's room so that the ringtone didn't wake her. Pulling it out, I saw that it was Whitney.

I hadn't spoken to my best friend since the previous weekend, so I hadn't had the chance to fill her in on everything going on at work. Eager to talk to her, I answered just before my voicemail picked up.

"Hello?" I walked downstairs and back to the kitchen.

"Hey," she greeted me. "What are you up to?"

The question itself didn't tell me anything, but there was a slight hesitation in Whitney's voice that made me frown. I put the call on speakerphone and placed the phone on the kitchen island while I poured myself a glass of wine.

"I'm just babysitting Gracie. Is everything okay with you?"

"Yeah, yeah." She hesitated for a moment. "I just need to tell you something…"

I took a sip of the sweet red wine and braced myself. Whatever it was, it sounded serious.

"I saw something on social media today," she finally said. "James is getting married."

I blinked. That was it? The urge to laugh bubbled up. "Oh my God, Whit. I thought someone died." I took another sip of wine before picking up the phone and heading to the living room couch. I settled in with my feet tucked underneath me.

Whitney exhaled, a long gust of worry leaving her. "So...you're not upset?"

"Absolutely not," I said emphatically. "All of that was years ago and I promise you I'm over it."

It was true. James was once the great unrequited love of my life and if I'd gotten this news two or three years ago, it would have devastated me. But I wasn't still in love with the man. We weren't even in contact these days.

Hearing about his wedding didn't reignite any of those old feelings, but it did remind me of how it felt to be cast aside, to feel like I wasn't good enough. I used to wonder what was wrong with me that made it so easy for James to keep me in the friend-with-benefits zone and never see me as more.

And stupidly, just for a second, my mind flickered to Liam. To waking up alone in that hotel room. To that same sting in my chest. But I forced myself to breathe through it, because I knew the situation wasn't the same.

Liam wasn't James. And what had happened with Liam wasn't a reflection of my worth. It was a reflection of *his* walls and his inability to stay when something felt real, and not a flaw in me.

"Well, I was a little concerned the news about

James would bother you, but I'm glad you're okay," Whitney said, bringing my attention back to our conversation. "Besides, you can do better than a playboy like him, anyway."

My mind betrayed me with an immediate image of Liam—broad shoulders, expensive suit, that focused stare he got when he was listening. The way he'd leaned toward me yesterday in his office, like kissing me was the most natural thing in the world.

Yeah, I sure knew how to pick them. Another man who didn't stick around when things got too intense. Another man with charm to spare and a past he seemingly wasn't over. A playboy? Not exactly. But unavailable? Absolutely.

I forced myself to shake it off before Whitney could hear every intrusive thought spiraling through my head. "Anyway," I said, clearing my throat and shifting gears fast, "Speaking of complicated men…there's something I haven't told you yet."

"Oh, no," she said, immediately alert. "What now?"

"Liam, the guy from my birthday?" I said, knowing she'd realize who I meant. "He's one of the investors working with GalvaTech."

There was a beat of stunned silence before Whitney practically shrieked, "Are you kidding me? What the hell. How did that even happen?"

"You think I planned it?" I muttered, rubbing my forehead. "I walked into the conference room and *surprise*, there he was."

Whitney groaned dramatically. "Of all the offices in New York, he had to walk into yours. Girl, that is a crazy coincidence."

I sighed. "Trust me, I know."

"Clearly, we have a lot to catch up on. Let's have dinner tomorrow night," Whitney insisted. "It feels like it's been forever since we've had some quality girl time."

I smiled. "You're on."

Maybe a night out was just what I needed to get my mind off a certain tall, dark, and sexy businessman. But even as I hung up the phone, I knew the odds of walking into work Monday morning unaffected by Liam Powers was nothing more than wishful thinking.

Because whatever was happening between us wasn't fading. It was temptation in a tailored suit, and resisting him was starting to feel impossible, even knowing that giving in might mean setting myself up for potential heartbreak.

CHAPTER ELEVEN

Liam

WHEN MY GOOD friend Henry texted me to join him for dinner and a night out, I didn't hesitate. After the week I'd had—long hours at GalvaTech, pretending not to be distracted by Morgan every time she walked past my office, nearly kissing her in a moment I still couldn't stop replaying in my mind—a couple of drinks in a loud nightclub sounded appealing. I needed something uncomplicated. Something that wasn't *her.*

And then Henry suggested sushi for dinner. My thoughts went straight to Morgan. Of course they did. To the way her eyes lit up when she'd mentioned this little place that she loved that was two blocks from the office.

Which was exactly how Henry and I ended up walking into *that* sushi restaurant on Saturday night.

The restaurant wasn't large, and most of the seating was around a horseshoe-shaped counter that took up the center of the space. A conveyor belt ran the length of the counter, carrying plates of various types of sushi that customers could grab at will. Chefs worked behind the counter replenishing trays and clearing empty plates with practiced skill and speed.

"Damn," Henry muttered beside me. "This place is slammed."

It was. Every stool was filled and for a second, I thought we'd have to leave or wait a ridiculously long time for a table.

"There—two spots," Henry said, pointing to the only empty seats at the counter. They were right at the start of the conveyor belt—prime real estate for the freshest plates.

We hurried over, and I pulled back the stool before sliding into place while Henry sat to my left. I didn't think to look at who was on my right until I was already settled.

When I glanced that way I saw familiar dark hair. Pink glossy lips. Wide, startled green eyes already locked on mine.

Well, shit.

"Are you stalking me or something?" Morgan asked, lips pursed tight.

I almost laughed at the accusation. "Are you serious?"

She lifted a shoulder, striving for casual, but I didn't miss the slight flush on her cheeks. "What am I supposed to think? Of all the restaurants in New York, you just happen to come into the one I'm at?"

"If I were stalking you, trust me, I'd be a hell of a lot smoother about it." I scanned the conveyor, then glanced back at her with a grin meant to ease the tension between us. "Running into you was pure luck. Or terrible timing, depending on how you feel about me tonight."

The corner of Morgan's mouth twitched with a smile, exactly what I'd been aiming for. "Seriously, though, there must be hundreds of sushi places in the city."

"Actually, there are approximately seven hundred forty-five of them," a woman sitting on Morgan's other side chimed in.

I recognized her from the night at the bar. She was the friend that checked in with Morgan before leaving.

I tipped my head curiously. "How do you know that?"

"Whitney is always sharing random facts," Morgan said, reaching for a plate with a dragon roll. "It's a whole thing with her. Never go up against her in a game of Trivial Pursuit."

"Noted." I snagged an Alaska roll for myself. "You told me about this place when I was setting up my office," I reminded her.

"Oh, right," she said, almost impishly.

"So, you two know each other?" Henry asked, his curious gaze bouncing between the two of us.

Morgan's eyes cut toward me, a silent warning to keep my reply G-rated.

"Oh, yeah," I drawled playfully. "We're old friends."

Morgan rolled her eyes. "We're coworkers," she explained.

Henry frowned at me. "Coworkers?"

"This is Morgan," I said, introducing her. "I'm working with her family's company."

"Ahh," he said, understanding that I meant I'd invested in their business. He shifted his attention to Morgan's friend. "And do you already know Liam?"

"Not exactly." She looked at me in a slightly disapproving way that told me she remembered me from that night at the bar, and was now judging me based on whatever Morgan had told her. "I'm Whitney."

"A beautiful name for a beautiful woman," Henry said smoothly.

Seriously? He's going to flirt with her while Morgan and I sat between them?

"You must be the charming one of this duo," Whitney said, flirting right back.

I wasn't sure if that was an insult or not, but Morgan snorted softly as she reached for another plate.

"I like to think that's the case," Henry replied, and I recognized that low, smooth-talking tone of voice he used when he zeroed in on a woman that he was interested in taking home.

That seemed like a terrible idea, considering her connection to Morgan. Things were complicated enough between us already, and I didn't want to risk more friction if our friends hooked up and someone got their feelings hurt. But I couldn't figure out a way to convey to him that Whitney should be off-limits.

So, I just pointed to the conveyor belt with my chopsticks. "You better eat while we're here. I doubt the nightclub will be serving food."

Henry grabbed a plate of sushi without looking and continued to flirt with Whitney. She responded in kind, and I found myself looking at Morgan, who had a helpless expression on her face.

"I guess you can't pretend I'm not here now," I teased.

She sighed, wiping her fingers on her napkin. "I'm sorry. I was rude when you sat down. It just…caught me off guard. Seeing you here, especially after we almost…" Her voice lowered, her shoulder touching mine as she leaned closer so our friends, who were absorbed in their own conversation, wouldn't hear. "Well, you know."

"Let's try and forget about that," I said too quickly, and regretted the words the moment they left my mouth.

She stilled, her fingers tightening around her chopsticks. "Right. Just like we're supposed to forget about the night we met," she replied.

I arched a brow. "I thought you said that night wasn't worth thinking about?" I shot back.

Her cheeks turned pink as I called her out on pretending she wasn't affected by our night together. "I did say that," she admitted, her voice quieter, more sincere. "But apparently that's easier said than done."

I held her gaze and was equally truthful. "I shouldn't think about it either, but I do." *Far too fucking much.*

The air between us felt charged. Heavy. Like if either of us said one more honest thing, something would shift in a way that we couldn't take back.

I cleared my throat and leaned back, trying to find solid ground. "I know this situation isn't ideal. Me being at GalvaTech, us having to work together. But, what if we call a truce?"

Her brows rose. "A truce?"

"Yeah." I kept my voice low, for her ears only. "The truth is, I don't want to forget about our night together because despite the way it ended, you were more than just a random hookup. I'm still attracted to you, clearly, and I think you feel the same."

"I do," she said, nodding slowly, cautiously. "What are you proposing, exactly?"

I exhaled a deep breath. "I'd like to think we can at least be friends."

The word immediately tasted wrong in my mouth. Friends didn't think about each other the way I thought about her. They didn't replay sexy conversations and heated moments in their head at two in the morning when they were tossing and turning and trying to sleep. They didn't notice every small detail about the other, like how her entire expression softened when she was being genuine with me. Or how her cheeks flushed whenever she tried to pretend she wasn't affected by our chemistry.

A friend definitely didn't remember how it felt to be deep inside her and the sounds she made when she came.

Morgan bit her lower lip, considering my proposal.

"You think being friends is possible?"

Honestly, the last thing I wanted was to be her damn friend. Not when I wanted to get my hands on her, explore every inch of her body, and watch her fall apart under me again.

"I do," I said, my voice low and rough. "Especially for the sake of working together." Which was a reminder of why I shouldn't be entertaining such sinful thoughts about her in the first place. Business and pleasure were a bad mix.

She glanced down at her chopsticks, rolling them between her fingers before glancing back at me. I caught the conflicting emotions in her eyes, indicating she was having the same struggle to keep things between us strictly professional.

"Okay," she finally said. "Friends it is."

She held out her hand to seal the deal we'd just made. The last time we'd shaken hands had been in that conference room, when she'd pulled away like I'd burned her. Now she was extending the gesture as a peace offering.

I took her hand, her skin warm and soft in my palm. My fingers closed around hers, and my body betrayed me instantly, desire pooling low. I should have let go immediately. Made it a quick, impassive handshake.

I didn't. Neither did she. I could feel her pulse fluttering at her wrist beneath my thumb.

"Friends," I finally said, my tone huskier than I'd intended.

Morgan's eyes darkened slightly, and I knew she felt it too. The connection we shared drew us together like gravity, no matter how sensible we tried to be about our situation.

Finally, she pulled her hand back and we resumed eating.

"So, how was babysitting last night?" Whitney asked Morgan, nudging her with her elbow to get her attention.

Morgan smiled at her friend. "It was fun. Gracie is so cute, and I can't wait until Becca has the baby. My little nephew will be here before we know it, and Gracie is so excited she's already talking about how she's going to help take care of the baby."

"Is this Parker's daughter?" I asked, remembering that Samuel mentioned his stepson had a little girl and a baby boy on the way.

"Yes." Morgan's eyes sparkled with delight. "She's three years old and a little angel."

"I'm close with my nieces, too," I said, sharing something we had in common—a tight family bond. "My brother Noah has a set of twins, and they are probably the coolest kids ever."

Morgan laughed, a much more light-hearted sound that seemed to fill my chest with warmth. "Not that you're biased or anything."

"Maybe," I admitted, and shrugged. "But you should meet these girls. Dylan is a girly girl. She loves dance and all things pink. And glitter. The girl is always covered in it, I swear. Every time I drive her somewhere, I'm vacuuming the stuff out of my car for days. And her sister Dakota is *so* smart, although she has this slightly disturbing habit of talking about death all the time."

Morgan tilted her head to the side. "Okay, you're going to have to explain that one."

"Her mom, Charlie, is an archeologist. Dakota completely idolizes her and is fixated on the human remains side of her mom's occupation. So, she's always dropping these random facts about death."

Morgan watched me for a moment, a smile on her lips. "Wow. Your face really lights up when you talk about them."

It struck me how easy things suddenly felt between us. A simple truce, and the tension from earlier had slipped away, replaced by something relaxed and comfortable. The moment felt almost like…a date.

Which it wasn't.

I reached for a plate coming toward us on the conveyor belt at the same exact moment Morgan reached for it, too. Our fingers brushed, and we both pulled away.

"You go ahead," I said, indicating that she should take the plate.

She grabbed the dish and slid two of the four sushi rolls onto mine before glancing at me with a smile. "We'll share."

And that made it feel even more like a date. The urge to lean in close to her again was difficult to resist, so I shoved a sushi roll into my mouth and turned to

Henry. While we finished eating, I talked to my friend about our favorite football teams—the Giants for me and the Buffalo Bills for him—while the girls chatted on my other side.

It was fully dark outside when we finished dinner and it was time to head to the club. I covered the bill for all four of us despite Morgan's protests, leaving a large tip for the staff to split as I slid off my stool.

I was ready to put distance between Morgan and me because being near her confused me…and made me crave things I swore I'd stopped believing in years ago. I was starting to feel emotions I hadn't allowed myself to entertain since Ivy. Like wanting to trust someone again, wanting to show the parts of myself I kept guarded. Wanting something real…and being terrified of what it would cost me if I truly opened myself up to her.

"Come on," I said to Henry. "Let's get going."

But my friend didn't pick up on the reason for my urgency. He took his time sliding off his stool and putting his jacket on, all while Morgan and Whitney were gathering their things, too. Then, he opened his big, fat mouth.

"Why don't you girls join us at the club?" he asked.

Fuck.

Morgan hesitated, but Whitney beamed at Henry. "That sounds like so much fun!"

"I don't know," Morgan said more hesitantly, glancing at her friend. "I thought this was supposed to be a girls' night."

"Yeah, but dancing and drinks and letting loose? That's exactly what I need to destress," Whitney said, while simultaneously batting her lashes and pouting. "Let's go, please?"

Morgan sighed, then glanced back at us. "Okay, sure, so long as we're not imposing."

"Not at all," Henry replied, his gaze on Whitney. "Right, Liam?"

Saying no wasn't an option, not without looking like an asshole, and the last thing I needed was to draw more attention to whatever was happening between us.

"Yeah," I said, forcing a smile that felt tighter than I wanted it to. "The more, the merrier."

Henry shot me a satisfied look, completely oblivious to the fact that he'd just thrown fuel on a fire I was barely managing to contain, despite my friend zone pact with Morgan.

I slid my hands into the pockets of my jacket, resigned to spending the night with the one woman who tested my self-control, and was completely off limits.

CHAPTER TWELVE

Morgan

I WASN'T THE type to party every weekend, but I was usually up for a good time whenever my closest friends suggested it. Tonight though, I had serious doubts about whether or not this was a good idea.

I was reluctant to accept Henry's invitation, but Whitney seemed excited about the idea, and I didn't want to let her down. I wasn't sure if she wanted to go because she liked Henry or if she was just eager to let loose a little. She had a serious and tiring job as a physical therapist at a hospital, so I knew that she preferred to enjoy her weekends as much as possible.

Whitney had driven us to the sushi restaurant, so she also drove to the club, following Liam's car so we'd end up at the same place. Traffic was heavy, typical of a New York Saturday night, and it took us about thirty minutes to get there, even though we were only traveling a few miles.

"So, are you mad that I accepted the invitation?" Whitney asked while we were in the car.

"No," I assured her, keeping my true feelings

about it to myself. "I wouldn't have agreed otherwise."

Whitney glanced at me quickly before looking back at the road. "It's just that despite everything, there still seems to be something between you and Liam."

I couldn't deny her observation, but I wasn't about to admit it out loud, either.

Whitney drummed her fingers on the steering wheel. "When I agreed to go to the club, I was kind of swept up in Henry's flirty personality, and I wasn't really thinking about your situation with Liam. We can go somewhere else if you'd like."

I placed a hand on her arm and squeezed. "It's fine, really."

She shot me a sideways look. "How are things going between you two at the office?"

Since we'd sat with Liam and Henry at the sushi restaurant, we hadn't had the chance for any kind of private conversation, or to discuss my working relationship with Liam. "Well, we almost kissed on Thursday afternoon."

Her eyes widened as she pulled into the parking lot behind the men. "Well, that's…something. What happened?"

"Absolutely nothing," I said quickly. "We were interrupted."

She grinned at me. "But will it happen again?"

I shook my head vehemently as Whitney parked her car across from Henry and Liam, and we watched them exit their vehicle. "No." The conviction in my voice might have been more for me than her.

Whitney tipped her head curiously. "Because you don't want it to, or because it's a bad idea?"

I groaned. "You always ask the hard questions."

"That's what friends are for. So, what's your answer?"

I sighed, and I realized that the guys were looking at us now, probably wondering why we were still sitting in the car. "A little bit of both," I admitted. "I'm still attracted to him, but I wish I wasn't. And, kissing him again is a *terrible* idea."

"Yeah," Whitney said, a sly smile on her lips. "But sometimes terrible ideas are the most satisfying ones."

"You are such a bad influence," I said, and laughed.

We exited the car and met up with the men. We didn't have to wait long to get inside. Liam slipped a large bill to the bouncer, and we bypassed the long line and stepped into the club's dark, pulsing interior.

The music was loud and there were people crowding in on all sides as we made our way farther into the club. Half of the space was a dance floor, and the rest was the bar area where there were tables and chairs as well as booths against the walls. Every seat was occupied and people were pressed up against the bar, trying to get the bartender's attention for a drink.

I started in that direction, but Liam gently grabbed my arm to stop me. "Henry will get the drinks while we try and find a table."

We gave Henry our drink orders and Liam placed a hand on my lower back and guided me forward. I thought that Whitney and I would go our separate way from the men once inside, but a table with four chairs emptied, and Liam ushered us over to it. I figured it would be rude to wander off now that he had secured us premium seating, and Henry had bought us drinks.

We settled in. I wore a red leather jacket over a black dress with strappy heels. I probably would have chosen something a little more revealing and done more with my make-up if I'd known we were going to a club, but I figured this was good enough for an impromptu night out. And, it wasn't like I was trying to impress anyone.

I stripped off my jacket and hung it on the back of my chair. Liam sat across from me at the table and when I glanced his way, his gaze was fixed on my chest. I raised my eyebrows and stared at him. It only took a couple of seconds for him to realize he'd been caught ogling me, but he didn't look the least bit contrite. His eyes were dark, direct, and appreciative.

A familiar heat rolled through me before I looked away and toward the dance floor where multi-colored lights flashed over the crowd.

"Here we go," Henry said as he returned with our drinks and set them on the table. He and Liam had ordered basic beers while Whitney and I had opted for fruity cocktails.

The DJ's music was too loud to allow for easy conversation, so we didn't talk much as we enjoyed our drinks. Whitney and I sang along to the music, popular pop and rock songs from the last decade, while Henry's gaze scanned the crowd like he was searching for his next fling. I hoped that Whitney wasn't too attached to the flirty guy.

I figured Liam would be doing the same thing, but every time I glanced his way, his eyes were on me. The intensity of his gaze made my entire body feel warm and restless. My breath hitched as memories of our night together flashed in my mind, of how it felt to be the object of his focused desire.

This has to stop.

We'd just agreed to a truce and set boundaries. To be friends. To keep things uncomplicated between us and professional at work. I knew if I allowed myself to be swayed by that heated stare, I would break every rule I'd made for myself when it came to this man.

I needed a distraction. Something, anything, that didn't involve imagining what he'd look like pressed against me in the shadows of this club.

"Excuse me," a deep voice said from behind me.

Turning in my chair, I found a man with shoulder-length blond hair and blue eyes looking at me with a smile on his lips. "Would you like to dance?"

Direct and good-looking. I liked both of those points. And he wasn't a complicated coworker that was driving me crazy.

"Yes," I said without pausing to even think about it.

I stood, allowing Blue Eyes to take my hand and lead me to the dance floor. I caught Liam's gaze as we passed by him, and I could have sworn I saw a surprising spark of jealousy flash in his copper-colored eyes.

Embrace the distraction, I reminded myself.

The DJ was playing a Bon Jovi song that half the dance floor was singing along to, and I joined them, shaking my hips and raising my arms in the air. I didn't hold myself back, singing and dancing and sending flirtatious smiles at the man that led me out here. He stayed close but mostly kept his hands to himself, aside from the occasional skimming of his fingers along my back or arms. He was respectful and didn't cross any lines so I didn't mind his subtle touch.

I had fun through the first two songs, but then Blue Eyes excused himself and left the dance floor. I guessed he wasn't that into me, but I was fine with that. I was still hung up on the last guy I met in a bar, and I didn't need to get attached to someone else. No pressure fun was better anyway.

I stayed on the dance floor, hoping that Whitney might join me, and I was only halfway through the next song when another man stepped up to me.

Immediately, he took the opportunity to get handsy. His palms landed on my hips, and he pulled me back until my ass was pressed against his groin. He started to grind into me, and I quickly stepped away. Spinning around, I saw a man with black hair, a smarmy smile on his face, and his eyes glassy from too much alcohol.

"Hands off," I shouted loud enough to be heard over the music.

His grin widened, but he lifted his hand like he was

being cooperative, which lasted all of about thirty seconds before his hands were back on my hips, fingers digging in uncomfortably hard.

I stiffened immediately and shoved his hands away. This time, I glared as I sidestepped several feet away and started dancing again, determined not to let one creep ruin my night. But the man was persistent, and clearly intoxicated. This time, he moved in front of me and reached around to grab my ass with both hands.

I gasped in outrage, and I was about to push against his chest to make him back off, but I didn't get the chance. He was ripped away from me so fast I staggered a step back.

My jaw dropped as Liam shoved the man to the ground, his face lined with rage. His eyes quickly swept over me, sharp and focused, not ogling like earlier but instead likely checking for injuries. Protective in a way that hit me straight in the chest.

Once he seemed satisfied that I was okay, he turned back toward the jerk, who was scrambling to his feet. Liam's jaw tensed, his fists clenched at his sides, and his eyes blazing with fury. A circle had formed around us, people eagerly watching, waiting to see what unfolded. Phones were already out, ready to record a fight.

My stomach twisted. I didn't want a scene. I didn't want Liam arrested or the star of some viral video of a club brawl that would remain on the internet long after this night was over.

Liam stepped toward the other man, and I grabbed

his arm. "Liam, I'm fine," I said, hoping to diffuse the situation.

"Fucker needs to learn to keep his hands to himself," he growled furiously.

The man stood upright again, and while a bit unsteady on his feet, he looked pissed. Thankfully, he remained in place, not brave enough to take a step forward. Not when Liam was several inches taller and probably had at least thirty pounds of muscle on him.

"He's not worth it." My voice shook. I hated that show of vulnerability, but adrenaline was fading fast, leaving me trembling all over. "Please, Liam, let's just go. He's not worth another second of our night."

The desperation in my voice must have penetrated his anger. He looked at me, seeing that I was barely holding it together, then glanced back at the other man. "You got lucky this time, asshole," Liam snarled at him, then turned away, taking me gently by the arm and leading me off the dance floor.

People parted to let us through, and while I was grateful that Liam had shown up when he had, embarrassment seeped into me. I was definitely rattled by the other man's grabby behavior and I just wanted to go home.

But when we got back to the table, it was empty.

"They're at the bar," Liam said, answering my unvoiced question.

He grabbed my jacket off the back of my chair and held it open for me to put my arms through, his gaze searching my face as his fingers grazed the side of my neck as he adjusted the collar.

"You okay?" he asked, his voice low and gruff, even as his thumbs gently skimmed along my jawline.

I nodded, swallowing hard. "Yeah. Thanks for…that." My words came out steadier than I felt, but I didn't step away, the proximity making it hard to ignore how his presence grounded me, even as it stirred up everything I'd been trying to push away.

His expression softened just a fraction. "I didn't like seeing him touch you like that." His tone was possessive and rough around the edges, and the way his eyes held mine made me shiver.

"I can handle myself," I assured him. "But, I'm glad you were there."

"Me, too," he replied, giving me a small nod, his anger mostly dissipated. "Come on, I'm getting you out of here."

Leaving was exactly what I wanted, but I couldn't just go. "I can't take off without letting Whitney know." Though, by the looks of things, she was once again flirting with Henry, oblivious to what just happened to me.

Liam took my hand and led me in their direction. When we reached them, he caught Henry's attention. "There was an incident on the dance floor. Some asshole got handsy with Morgan. I'm taking her home."

Whitney turned immediately, her eyes widening with concern as she looked me over. "Are you okay?"

"I'm fine," I said quickly, squeezing her arm to reassure her. "Just an asshole who wouldn't take no for an answer. Liam handled it. But I'm ready to call it a night. I'm a little shaken up."

She frowned, glancing between me and Liam, her worry clear. "I can come with you. We don't have to stay."

I shook my head. "No, really," I insisted, managing a small smile. "You should enjoy the rest of the night. You deserve to unwind."

Whitney hesitated, biting her lip, but then nodded. "Okay, but if you need anything, call me. And be safe." She pulled me into a quick hug, whispering, "Text me details later."

When we pulled apart I rolled my eyes at her. There would be no *details* to share. Not the kind she was insinuating, anyway.

Henry clapped Liam on the shoulder. "I'll keep an eye on Whitney."

I smirked at my friend. "I'm sure he will," I said, leaning close to say the words in her ear. "Text *me* later."

She just grinned.

Then Liam was guiding me toward the exit. We didn't speak as we walked across the parking lot toward his vehicle. His hand stayed on my lower back, steady and reassuring. I told myself he was just making sure I was okay. That it didn't mean anything other than offering me comfort.

But the warmth of his palm through my dress, the way he stayed close, felt like more than just concern.

His touch was both protective and unmistakably intimate. His attentive focus on me felt like something we were both still trying to pretend wasn't real.

I slid into the passenger seat of Liam's sports car. I didn't know much about makes and models, but I was aware this vehicle was high end from the leather seats and woodgrain trim. The interior smelled like coffee and Liam, his cologne making the interior space feel more intimate.

I gave him my address, and he put it into the GPS built into the dash. We made the drive to my building in a comfortable silence, and as he wound his way through the city, I stared out the window, trying not to replay the scene on the dance floor. But it kept looping in my head, the way Liam stepped in without hesitation, the command in his voice, and the way he'd positioned his body between mine and imminent danger like his automatic instinct was to protect me.

I shouldn't have liked the feeling as much as I did. I shouldn't have felt that little jolt of heat at the possessiveness in his eyes. We'd made a pact. A truce to remain friends and keep things professional. But nothing about tonight felt even remotely simple or casual.

He was making it very, very difficult to keep those promises, and the worst part was…I didn't know what to do about it. My head knew the rules we had agreed to and why we'd drawn those lines in the first place. But my heart? Well, my heart was ready to ignore those boundaries, wanting things I shouldn't desire.

And I had no idea how I was going to handle the dichotomy of feelings.

When he pulled up in front of my apartment building and parked at the curb, he switched off the engine and turned to me before I could get out of the car. He hadn't parked near a streetlight, but I could still see the intensity in his eyes.

"Are you sure you're okay after what happened at the club?" he asked, his voice roughened with residual worry.

There was that concern again, and I gave him a reassuring smile. "Yes. I'm good. Thank you again for protecting me even when you didn't have to."

"Of course. He needed to be taught a lesson," he said, his tone hardening for a second. "A real man doesn't touch a woman unless she wants him to. And I most definitely *did* have to step in."

His eyes dropped to my lips and the air in the car felt thicker, charged with everything we'd been dancing around since the restaurant. And the realization hit me hard—I wanted *this* man to touch me. Badly.

Liam reached out slowly, his fingers skimming along my jawline, light but deliberate. A shiver ran through me, making my skin tingle. That simple caress shifted everything. The awareness between us spiked, the attraction we'd both tried to deny pulling us in like it had its own magnetic force field. His gaze met mine again, and I didn't pull away.

I was so tired of denying what I wanted, and before I changed my mind, I leaned across the console, closing the gap between us. He didn't pull back when our lips met, soft at first, but igniting fast. His mouth was warm and insistent, tasting faintly of beer from the club. I pressed closer, one hand finding his shoulder, the other sliding to the back of his neck, pulling him in. He responded immediately, his lips parting mine, the kiss deepening with a hunger that made my head spin and my pulse race.

The desire between us built quickly, tongues tangling, breaths mingling in the tight, dark space of the car. I nipped at his bottom lip, and he groaned low, the arousing sound vibrating through me. My body arched toward his, desperate for more contact, the console digging into my side but not enough to stop me. His hand cupped my face, thumb tracing my cheek, while the other gripped my waist, urging me closer.

From there, things seemed to spiral out of control. He broke the kiss just long enough to mutter, "Come here," in a rough and commanding tone.

Strong hands guided me over the console, dragging me onto his lap. I straddled him, my dress riding up my thighs as my knees settled on either side of his hips. The steering wheel at my back forced me closer to Liam, until our bodies were flush. My breasts crushed against his chest, and the hard length of his cock pressing between my legs sent a jolt of need straight to my core.

We crashed back into the kiss, heated and urgent now. With a deep groan, his mouth claimed mine, teeth clashing as one hand tangled in my hair, tilting my head for better access. The other skimmed up my thigh, slow and teasing, pushing beneath the hem of my dress. His warm fingers traced the edge of my panties before slipping beneath.

I gasped into his mouth as he stroked my slick pussy, his thumb rubbing my clit with just the right pressure. I tilted my hips, allowing him to slide two fingers inside me, curving them to hit that spot that made my toes curl.

I was grateful we were in this dark spot, hidden from prying eyes and probably fogging up the windows. We shouldn't be doing this considering all the reasons why this was a bad idea, but everything about Liam felt so good, so right. His touch was confident, stroking me in that perfect rhythm as I rocked against his hand. I could feel his erection straining against me, hard and thick, and I ground down on it instinctively, the friction making him growl against my lips.

The pleasure built fast, coiling tight in my belly. His fingers pumped deeper, his thumb working my clit in firm circles, and I broke the kiss to bury my face in his neck, moaning softly. My hips moved with his own upward thrusts, chasing the edge, every stroke of his hand sending sparks through me.

My internal muscles clenched against his fingers and I came hard, shuddering against him. Waves of bliss rolled through me, my thighs trembling, breath hitching as I rode out the pleasure, shamelessly grinding down on his lap for more.

He tensed beneath me, his free hand gripping my hip hard, and a raw groan rumbled in his chest as his hips jerked erratically. His stiff cock was aligned with my pussy and I felt him pulse against me, growling deep in his throat as he came too, right there in his pants, while I was still coming down from my orgasm.

We both sat there afterward, breathing hard, chests heaving in the dark car. I was shocked, my mind reeling from how fast things had escalated, and how intense it had been.

"*Fuck*," he rasped, his head dropping back against his seat.

I pulled back slightly, still straddling him, my hands on his shoulders. His hooded gaze looked up at me, and a slow smile curved my lips.

"Did you just…come?" I asked, because, well, that was hot as fuck.

A rueful grin tugged at his lips despite the heat still in his gaze. "Yeah," he admitted, his hands sliding down to rest on my thighs. "Haven't done that since I was a fucking teenager."

I laughed softly, but his expression grew more serious. The warmth in his eyes shifted, giving way to something more conflicted and my stomach dropped.

He exhaled slowly. "What are we doing, Morgan?"

The question made something in my chest tighten. The high of what we'd just done was still pulsing through my body, but reality pressed in just as fast.

"I don't know," I whispered. It was the truth. My heart was racing for a hundred different reasons, and not one of them made sense.

Liam closed his eyes for a moment, like he needed to collect himself. When he opened them, the heat lingered, but it was softer now, layered with something more cautious.

"Jesus, Morgan," he said, his voice threaded with frustration and uncertainty. "I'm trying to do the right thing here."

I swallowed hard, feeling the weight of his words. "Are you putting me back in the friend zone?" I tried to keep my tone light, but there was a hint of vulnerability beneath that I couldn't hide.

He huffed out a strained laugh. "That's what I *should* do," he said reluctantly. "This could get complicated. We work together. We have a business relationship. If something goes wrong…I don't want to screw that up for either of us."

His words weren't dismissive. They were real, thoughtful, and laced with the same frustration and desire I felt. I could see the internal tug-of-war in his eyes, and I understood where he was coming from. This wasn't just about *us*. He was a business man who'd invested millions into my father's company, and I was adult enough to acknowledge that neither of us could predict what could potentially happen between us in the future.

I nodded, even though a small ache bloomed in my chest. "I get it. I do. It's confusing." My voice softened. "*I'm* confused. As much as I want you, the work stuff makes it tricky."

I saw the relief on his face that I wasn't angry or hurt. He cupped my cheek gently, just his fingertips, like he was afraid that too much contact would pull us right back into the spiral. "I don't want to hurt you," he said quietly. "And I don't want to mess up whatever is happening between us."

He didn't elaborate on that, but we both knew that our attraction, connection, and chemistry was off the charts and clearly not something we could ignore, no matter how hard we'd already tried to do so.

"I don't want that either," I replied, my hands resting on his chest, not ready to break the connection just yet.

"Let's just...slow this down," he suggested. "Figure it out without rushing."

"Okay," I agreed, knowing it was for the best.

I started to move off him, and he helped me back into the passenger seat. His hands stayed on me a moment longer than needed, sliding from my waist to my hips in a way that felt reluctant, like he was fighting the urge to pull me back onto his lap. I didn't take it as rejection. I recognized his restraint, the kind that told me he wanted more but was trying not to rush whatever this was between us. Because other things were at stake.

"Are we good?" he asked, and the concern I heard in his voice made it impossible to doubt his good intentions.

"Yeah, we are," I murmured, giving him a smile.

His eyes dropped to my lips for a beat, like the idea

of another kiss was still too tempting. "Yeah, we will be," he said quietly. "We'll figure this out."

His words were meant to reassure, but I didn't think either of us really believed getting through this and *figuring things out* would be that simple.

CHAPTER THIRTEEN

Liam

BY MUTUAL AGREEMENT, the following Monday at the office we were back to being professional, no mention of what happened in my car Saturday night. And even though I'd been the one to establish that "let's slow things down" suggestion, I fucking hated it.

Parker and Samuel had joined us for that morning's meeting, and Morgan sat across the conference table from me, facing the screen she'd set up for her PowerPoint presentation as she talked through the new product launch schedule for the next few months and her marketing ideas, her tone all business. Her hair was pulled back into a sleek ponytail, bringing my attention to her pretty face and features. She wore a navy blazer over a white blouse, looking every bit the competent marketing director. Polished, confident, and well put together.

Despite my best intentions, every time she spoke my eyes drifted to her lips, remembering the taste of her mouth when she'd leaned across the console in my car and kissed me. Of how she'd climbed onto my lap like she belonged there. How goddamn hard it had been to pull back instead of following her upstairs and losing myself in her for the rest of the night.

Driving away had been the hardest decision I'd made in years, even if it had been the right thing to do. We had this investment deal hanging over us, the launch timelines, the whole business partnership. Screwing that up wasn't an option. Neither was hurting Morgan again with a rash decision that was based solely on lust and desire.

"…and for the influencer rollout, I was thinking we could tie in some user-generated content to build buzz before the official drop," she said, pointing to the slide on the screen.

I nodded in agreement, as did Samuel. "Sounds solid. What about the timeline for the beta testers?" I asked.

She dove into the details with enthusiasm, outlining the various phases, but I was only half listening. My thoughts kept circling back to her. To us. It wasn't just the physical chemistry, though that mutual attraction was impossible to ignore. It was the connection we had made during our sushi dinner when we talked about our families, and how comfortable I was with her when neither one of us had our guard up. It was the way she'd look at me after our conversation in the car, understanding in her eyes when I said we needed to slow down. There had been no drama. No demands. That kind of maturity drew me in deeper and made me wonder if she could be something more.

Something real.

And just like our first night together, that possibility scared the shit out of me.

I was quickly realizing that Morgan Starling wasn't someone I could handle with detachment like I was used to. She was already so much more than that. She represented a possibility. A risk. A door I wasn't sure I was brave enough to open and step through. And if I was honest with myself, I was afraid of what might happen if I did.

My last relationship had imploded because I hadn't been enough. Ivy hadn't said it that way, but with distance came clarity, and I knew that was truth. She'd been lonely. Neglected. Relegated to whatever scraps were left after twelve-hour days and the nonstop grind of Wall Street had drained every ounce of energy I had. She'd gotten the rushed, distracted version of me. A quick dinner here and there, half-assed conversations while I constantly checked emails, cancelling plans because work always took priority. And romance, well, that became non-existent because I'd been too exhausted to nurture that part of our relationship.

So, she'd sought affection elsewhere. And yeah, I knew that decision was wrong and on her. She'd lied, cheated, and shattered what trust we had. She should have talked to me instead of jumping into bed with someone else.

But I wasn't completely innocent in creating the cracks that had formed in our relationship before she'd strayed. I hadn't listened. I didn't notice her unhappiness. I hadn't shown up the way a partner deserved. I should have seen the signs before it all blew up in my face. So, upon finding her with another man, my anger had been tangled up with guilt because I hadn't been blameless in the situation.

Despite everything, the breakup left me shattered. Guarded and unwilling to risk that kind of pain again. But Morgan…she was different. Smart, driven, with a quiet strength that matched mine. But if I dove in too fast, I feared I'd repeat the same mistakes—burying myself in work, leaving her with leftovers, and watching it all fall apart.

I didn't want to hurt her like that. Hell, I didn't want to get hurt again, either. So, if I was going to pursue her, I needed to make sure I was doing it for all the right reasons. That I was able to make her a priority without risking the business investment Simon and I had made with GalvaTech.

As she wrapped up her presentation, I forced myself to tune back in.

"I like the phasing approach," I said, complimenting her on how well she'd balanced the timeline, because I'd heard that much of her presentation. "Keeps the momentum going without overcommitting to a singular campaign before we test the messaging."

She smiled at me, a small, professional one, but there was a flicker of something warmer and more intimate underneath. "Agreed. I'm glad you approve. We can refine the details over the next few months."

"Great job, as always," Samuel chimed in. "You two seem to have everything pretty well handled and dialed in."

Parker murmured his agreement. He hadn't said much since the meeting started, his expression a bit pained as he'd shifted uncomfortably in his chair throughout the presentation. I chalked up his lack of input to his back injury flaring up.

The meeting wrapped, and as everyone filed out, I lingered, gathering my things slower than needed. Morgan did too, her gaze occasionally meeting mine. Part of me wanted to drag her off to my office, lock the door, and pick up where we'd left off Saturday. But no. If this was going to happen—and fuck, I really wanted to try with Morgan—I needed to do it right. Slowly. Meaningfully. Give us time to build something solid and real. She deserved that. We both did.

"So, I think we should work out a plan for building anticipation about the charger leading up to the launch," Morgan said, her mind clearly still in business mode as she straightened her notes, then looked up at me with that focused energy I found ridiculously attractive. "Maybe brainstorm some ideas for that."

I nodded, though I was one step ahead of her in that regard. "I had the same thought so I called in a few favors and was able to get GalvaTech signed up for CES."

Morgan's eyes widened in surprise. "Seriously? The Consumer Electronics Show in Vegas?"

I grinned at her, enjoying her bright, infectious

smile. “Do you know of any other CES?”

She playfully pressed a hand to her chest, feigning a dramatic swoon. “Be still my heart,” she teased, as if I’d given her a romantic present, and maybe for her, this was something that meant more than flowers or candy or jewelry—this was tailored to who she was, the marketing director with big ideas and even bigger ambitions. “That’s quite a feat, considering how late it is in the year and the first week of January is right around the corner. The show books up years in advance.”

“I know.” I crossed my arms with a satisfied nod.

“I’ve never been, but I’ve always wanted to go,” she said, closing her laptop once she shut down the presentation slides. “Having GalvaTech there is a big deal.”

It definitely was. “It’ll be great exposure,” I agreed.

Excitement sparked in her eyes. “I’m impressed. I can’t believe you got us into the largest annual trade show in the U.S.”

I tipped my head. “Impressed enough to forgive me for being completely useless in our meeting?”

She blinked at me. “You were not useless.”

“Oh, I absolutely was,” I countered, lowering my voice just a notch. “You could have presented the annual budget in interpretive dance and I would’ve nodded along like it made perfect sense.”

Her lips twitched as she tried, and failed, to keep a straight face. “Is this your way of admitting you were distracted?”

"Painfully," I confessed with a sigh.

Amusement flickered across her features, softening the professional edge she'd been maintaining all morning. "Well," she said lightly, "maybe you'll pay better attention at CES."

I arched a brow. "Are you planning to hold me accountable?" I asked, enjoying our flirtatious banter. Now that we'd eliminated the tension between us, this back-and-forth felt easy and natural. Light, fun, and full of promise.

"Someone has to," she teased. "Can't have you wandering off because a shiny new prototype catches your eye."

I held her gaze from across the table. "You're assuming prototypes are my weakness," I said, the words carrying just enough implication to make her bite her bottom lip.

"Oh?" she asked, her voice a bit breathless. "And what *is* your weakness?"

Dangerous question, considering the real answer was standing right in front of me. "Guess you'll have to come to Vegas to find out."

"Is that an invitation?" she asked huskily.

The corner of my mouth twitched with a smile. "As if you'd miss out on going."

She laughed, the sound soft and warm and intimate between us. "You're right. When do we leave?"

"It's still six weeks away, but we're looking at the first week of January," I said, casually strolling around the table to her side, but still maintaining a respectable distance just in case anyone walked by and glanced into the conference room. "We'll probably be there for four or five days total."

"Four or five days." She said it slowly, like she was considering what that meant. "In Vegas. Together."

"With the rest of the team," I added, though we both knew that wasn't really the point.

"Right. The team." Her eyes held mine, and I didn't miss the mischievous glint there. "Very professional."

"Extremely professional," I echoed, matching her tone, but my hands itched to reach out and touch her. Which I resisted, of course.

"Nothing unprofessional will happen whatsoever."

I shoved my hands into my pants pockets, fighting a smile. "Absolutely not."

"Good." She picked up her laptop and tucked it under her arm, but she didn't move right away. "Because we have boundaries now."

"Very firm boundaries."

"Exactly." She paused, her fingernails drumming once against the laptop. "Although Vegas is pretty far from New York."

"Three time zones," I said, staring at her mouth.

She licked her bottom lip. "And what happens in Vegas…"

"Stays in Vegas," I finished, my voice lower.

She smiled in a way that made my pulse spike. "Just making sure we're on the same page."

I swallowed back a groan. "Morgan, we're supposed to be taking this slow. Remember?"

"I do remember." She tilted her head slightly, studying me. "But you're the one who booked us a trip to Vegas."

"For work," I countered.

"Mm-hmm," she said, clearly amused. "And I'm sure you were thinking very professional thoughts when you considered that both of us would be going."

I had been. Mostly. The fact that it would mean several days of seeing her outside of the office, working closely together, maybe finding moments alone—that had been entirely coincidental. At least, that's what I was telling myself.

"I was thinking about the product launch," I said.

"Sure you were." She rolled her eyes playfully, but her smile was soft and affectionate.

"I'm serious," I insisted, though I couldn't hide my grin.

"I believe you." She was trying not to laugh now. "You're very serious. Very focused on work."

"I am."

"So focused that you couldn't pay attention during my presentation this morning?" she pointed out with a triumphant gleam in her eyes.

I opened my mouth. Closed it. She had me there.

Her smile widened. "That's what I thought."

I narrowed my gaze, just a bit. "You're enjoying this."

"Maybe a little." She exhaled a breath that wasn't quite steady. "Actually, it's nice to know I'm not the only one who's distracted."

"You're distracted?" I asked, even though I could see it in her eyes. The same desire I felt.

"Completely." Her voice softened. "I spent all of Sunday thinking about Saturday night."

Heat spread through me at the admission, the memory of her in my lap making my dick twitch very inappropriately considering where we were. "Yeah?" I had to work to keep my voice steady and my hands to myself.

"Yeah." She bit her bottom lip, and I had to force myself not to stare at her mouth. "And then I came to work this morning determined to be professional and focus on the launch, and you were sitting across from me at this conference table looking at me like…"

"Like what?" I asked, stepping closer without meaning to.

"Like you wanted to do very unprofessional things."

I didn't bother denying it. "Would it help if I apologized?"

"Not really," she said with a small, warm smile. "Because I was having the same unprofessional thoughts."

We stood there, the space between us charged with everything we weren't saying. Everything we were trying not to do. Yet the emotional undercurrent felt solid, like we were both invested in exploring this carefully. Together.

I exhaled a deep breath. "This slow thing is going

to be harder than I thought," I admitted.

"For me, too. But, I think it's the right call. We should figure out what this is before we...you know." She gestured vaguely, her expression a mix of amusement and sincerity.

"Jump back into my car for another make-out session?" I suggested, keeping it light, but the heated memory flashed between us.

Her cheeks flushed pink once again. "Something like that."

"For the record," I said quietly. "I'm very interested in figuring out what this is."

"Good." Her smile turned genuine, less teasing. More real. "Because so am I."

She headed for the door and I watched her go, trying not to notice the way her skirt hugged her curves—her ass, especially. Then she was gone, leaving me standing there with a smile I couldn't quite get rid of, along with the unsettling, impossible to ignore feeling that I was already in deeper than I'd planned.

THE NEXT TWO weeks blurred into a steady rhythm of deadlines, strategy meetings, and long nights in the office. The charger launch was picking up speed, CES planning was in full swing—booth designs approved, demo units prepped, and travel logistics sorted for the team—and somehow, despite the chaos, things with Morgan felt easy and natural.

We hadn't crossed any lines since that night in my car, not even a kiss, but the flirting hadn't stopped and it felt suspiciously like…dating. I liked getting to know her piece by piece in her established environment. Learning all those small, intimate details about her, a person that I genuinely liked—what made her laugh, what fired her creativity, watching how she talked with her hands when she got excited about something.

Those light-hearted, playful moments threaded through our days. She'd roll her eyes when I triple-checked meeting times. I'd tease her about her obsession with color-coded spreadsheets. She'd pretend not to be affected when I leaned over her shoulder to look at her computer screen so she could show me one of her graphs. One morning, she'd complimented me on my tie with a sexy gleam in her eyes, and I spent the rest of the day trying not to imagine her tugging on it.

The sexual tension was there, simmering just beneath the surface of every conversation, every shared laugh, every moment our eyes met across the office or the conference table. There was something about the way she'd show up at my office door in the morning with coffee, knowing exactly how I liked it. The way we'd debate marketing strategies and product features, and how she would call me out when my ideas were too over the top and unrealistic. The way she'd stay late at night at the office just because I was working, sharing a take-out meal with me, even though she could have gone home hours ago.

It felt like we were building something between us.

Laying a foundation that could actually hold weight in the real world. And I wanted that. I wanted to take her out to a romantic dinner. Wanted to walk her home and kiss her goodnight at her door. I wanted to do this the right way—slow and intentional, proving that this wasn't just about our physical attraction, as tempting as that was.

But there was no opportunity. Between everything moving at a swift pace at GalvaTech and Simon needing my time and advice on hammering out the final details of the Stark, Inc. investment—which required endless calls, negotiations over equity shares, and due diligence that ate into every spare minute—my days were stretched impossibly thin.

But things between myself and Morgan seemed solid and all that flirty banter, the shared looks and inside jokes, was creating this delicious sexual tension that made every interaction electric, like a slow burn promising so much more once we finally let it ignite.

It was only a matter of time before it did. Because somehow, I felt myself falling deeper into whatever this was becoming between us.

Thanksgiving slipped by in the midst of it all. I spent the day with my family, the usual chaos of a turkey dinner and football and playing with my nieces. Even then, my mind kept drifting back to Morgan, wondering how her holiday went and fighting the urge to text her something flirty that might blur our self-imposed lines.

We were back in the office after the long weekend,

hitting the ground running refining prototypes, getting marketing strategies locked in, and signing off on vendor contracts. The pace was relentless, but necessary. CES was approaching, the launch calendar was tight, and every department was grinding hard to make sure nothing slipped through the cracks.

Mid-week, I called Parker and Samuel into a meeting to discuss a decision I'd made.

As we settled around the conference table, I couldn't help noticing that Parker looked ragged. His expression was pale, and he seemed quieter and more withdrawn. I could only assume that his back pain was acting up again.

"I won't keep you two long," I said, glancing between the two men, and got right to business. "I want to increase the budget for marketing."

To my surprise, Parker frowned, the crease between his brows sharp and immediate. "I don't think we should make that a priority right now," he muttered, his tone edged with irritation as he picked at his fingernails.

Samuel blinked at Parker, just as thrown as I was by Parker's unexpected objection. "Why not, son?"

Parker hesitated before answering. "Because the manufacturing costs are already massive, and it's not the right time to throw more money at marketing."

"The money I've invested should be enough to cover the manufacturing and the increase in the marketing budget," I pointed out, then went on to justify my reasons. "Industry research shows that competitors are pouring money into visibility. If GalvaTech doesn't invest now, they risk becoming invisible in a sector where early brand recognition and consumer awareness is everything. I want GalvaTech positioned as a front-runner, not a quiet newcomer."

"That makes sense," Samuel said, supporting my idea.

Parker's eyes shifted away from me, jaw flexing once before he clamped down on whatever else he wanted to say. Unease curled in my stomach, not enough to call him out, but enough to make me pay attention. I didn't know him well enough to understand the sudden pushback, or the tension rolling off him in waves.

Still, he didn't argue further, and right now, that was what mattered. We had a product to launch, and I needed him aligned and working with me, not against me, so we could make this launch a success.

The meeting wrapped quickly after that. Parker practically bolted for the door. I rose to leave as well, but Samuel's hand landed gently on my arm to stop me.

"I want to thank you for all that you're doing for the company," he said with a warm, fatherly smile. "I can feel us moving closer to success every day. I also wanted to invite you to my home for a dinner party this Saturday with the family. My wife, Faith, would love to meet you. GalvaTech has always been a family business, and now that you've invested your time and money into it, I guess that makes you an honorary member."

He chuckled, and I was touched by the thoughtfulness of his invitation. Most of the other companies I'd worked with kept things formal and transactional, and I appreciated the way he valued me as part of the company.

"I'd love to come to dinner," I said.

Samuel smiled again, genuine and grateful, and as I walked out, I realized I wasn't just invested in GalvaTech anymore. I was invested in the people. In Morgan. Maybe more than I should be.

CHAPTER FOURTEEN

Morgan

I STOOD INSIDE my walk-in closet, staring at my options like they might suddenly arrange themselves into the perfect outfit.

It was just dinner, I told myself. My father had invited Liam as a gesture of appreciation and gratitude. A completely casual and thoughtful overture…except nothing about the way I was starting to feel for Liam felt even remotely neutral anymore.

Sighing, I pulled out a simple and classic black dress, then put it back. Too formal. Tried a sweater and jeans. Too relaxed. A silk blouse and tailored pants. Too professional.

Ugh. "Get it together," I muttered to myself.

This was ridiculous. I'd never had trouble picking an outfit before. But then again, I'd spent the past few weeks in a constant state of anticipation, wondering when Liam and I would finally cross that line we'd been dancing around since that night in his car. Tonight, I wanted to feel that spark between us a little more.

We hadn't kissed again. Hadn't touched beyond the occasional brush of hands or his palm at my lower back when he'd walked me to my car like a gentleman after a late night at the office. Whatever we were developing felt easy in a way I hadn't expected. Like we'd skipped past the awkward getting-to-know-you phase and landed somewhere deeper. Somewhere that mattered and felt real.

My cellphone buzzed on my dresser. I picked it up and saw a text from Whitney.

Please tell me you're not overthinking what to wear.

I laughed, because only a best friend would know me that well after learning I was going to be seeing Liam at a family dinner.

I typed back, *I have no idea what you're talking about.*

Liar. Just wear the red dress. The one that makes your boobs look so damn good they should come with a warning label.

I grinned and shook my head. *It's a family dinner.*

With a man you're clearly into. Wear. The. Dress. You've been doing the slow burn thing for weeks now. Maybe it's time to turn up the heat a little.

I bit my lip, staring at the red dress hanging at the back of my closet. It was one of my favorites. Fitted to my curves, but not too tight. Sophisticated and subtle enough for a family dinner, but tempting enough for Liam.

Fine, I finally responded. *The red dress it is.*

That's my girl. Now go ruin his self-control.

I pulled the dress from the closet and laid it on the

bed. I took a deep breath. It was just dinner with my family…and Liam. Who looked at me like I was the only person in the room even when we were surrounded by people. Who made me feel things I wasn't sure I was ready to name yet.

I slipped into the dress and looked at myself in the mirror. Whitney was right. My boobs looked fantastic. And the fit was perfect, hugging my curves in all the right places without being too much.

I looked good. More than that, I felt confident and beautiful.

I left for my parents' house, and when I arrived Parker and Becca were already there, but Liam's car wasn't in the driveway yet. My stepmom, Faith, greeted me at the door, her kind brown eyes lighting up as she immediately pulled me into a warm hug.

When my father married Faith just three years after my mother's death, I wasn't exactly thrilled. It wasn't just that a short period of time had passed, that had worried me. I'd been eleven at the time, and I'd been afraid of how the family dynamic would change. I had a close relationship with my father, and he was all I had. I'd been wary that Faith would come between us.

But that didn't happen. She wasn't the evil stepmother that Disney movies had taught me to fear. Faith was kind and patient with me. She didn't try to replace my mother, but she filled the emptiness that was left behind in the best way she could. She became my friend and mentor, someone that helped me through the difficult years of puberty and all of the drama that came with growing from a girl into a woman.

Nowadays, we still had a close relationship.

"Look at you," she said, her gaze taking in my outfit as we broke apart. "Are you trying to impress someone with that dress?"

Maybe our relationship was *too* close. It clearly allowed her to see too much. It didn't help that she was a psychologist; her profession made her great at observing a person's behavior and deriving meaning from it.

"No," I said, smoothing down imaginary wrinkles in my dress. "It's a dinner party, Faith. Isn't that a reason to look nice?"

"Of course," she agreed with a soft laugh, though her eyes twinkled with unspoken suspicion before she headed to the kitchen to check on dinner.

I walked into the dining room to greet everyone. A moment later the doorbell rang and Gracie ran by me on her way to answer the door, her curls bouncing while my dad chased after her.

"I get the door!" she yelled.

My dad laughed, loving his role as a granddad. "Slow down, young lady. You're too young to answer the door."

I couldn't stop my smile. If the new baby ended up being as rambunctious as that little girl, Parker and Becca would have their hands full.

Moments later, my father guided Liam into the dining room, and just like that, the air shifted and butterflies fluttered in my stomach.

Gracie stared up at him like she'd discovered a superhero. "You're tall," she announced, her little voice full of awe.

Liam laughed softly, and the sweet and kind look he gave my niece was enough to melt my heart. But then his gaze lifted to mine.

The way he looked at me wasn't overt. It wasn't inappropriate. But it was undeniably appreciative, his eyes sweeping over me in a single controlled pass, like he was trying not to stare but couldn't help himself. A shiver raced up my spine and my pulse seemed to trip all over itself. The intensity in his eyes reminded me of every charged moment we'd shared since that make-out session in his car, making me ache for more.

He cleared his throat lightly and glanced away, but not before I saw that same awareness I'd been trying to ignore for weeks.

"It's lovely to meet you, Liam," Faith said as she stepped forward to shake his hand.

Liam smiled at her. "The pleasure is all mine. Thank you for having me."

Becca entered the dining room a moment later, also introducing herself. I wondered if she'd remember seeing him at the bar the night of my birthday party, but there was no recognition in her eyes.

Liam clearly remembered her, but he didn't say a word as we all settled in for dinner. Gracie loved meeting new people and boldly grabbed Liam's hand, insisting that he sit next to her at the table. Parker was already seated on the other side of her booster seat, and Becca raised an eyebrow.

"You don't want to sit by me?" Becca asked in a playfully teasing voice.

"You sit by Daddy," Gracie said as Parker strapped her into her booster seat.

There was laughter around the table, and I slid into a chair across from Liam. Once dinner was on the table, Faith sat next to me with my dad on her other side. It was like any of the other countless family meals we'd had, but it felt completely different because Liam was here, and every time I looked up, his eyes were already on me.

Gracie chattered most of the meal, directing her questions and observations toward Liam. I doubt that he expected to spend this whole meal engaging with a toddler, but he was patient and kind with her the whole time.

"Why do you have brown hair?" she asked randomly, and he smiled as he thought about the answer.

"I guess it's because my dad has brown hair," he said, and Gracie's eyes went to Parker. She looked shocked, as if it never occurred to her before that her own brown hair might have come from him.

"I have to wonder if the new baby will look like you too," Becca said to Parker, rubbing a hand over her pregnant belly.

Parker touched one of Becca's curls and smiled at her. "I wouldn't mind a little blond baby."

"Are you guys excited to add a new member to the family?" Liam asked.

"Oh, yes," Becca said, nodding enthusiastically. "We've always wanted two kids, and now our family will be complete. Next, we need to find a bigger house for all of us."

She laughed lightly, but my eyes shifted to Parker. Was it my imagination, or did his expression tense at the mention of them buying a new home?

Gracie chose that moment to interrupt the conversation, tugging on Liam's sleeve to tell him all about the picture of a rainbow she drew earlier in the day, and it was amazing how much she had to say about it. Liam gave her his attention once again, no hint of boredom or impatience in his expression.

As other conversations went on around the table, I couldn't seem to stop myself from watching him interact with my niece, as subtly as possible. This wasn't like when I stared at him at the office and fantasized about being intimate with him. That was physical attraction and on a whole other level.

My *heart* was drawn into this. I could feel it ache as I saw this soft side of him.

When dessert came around—a small dish of chocolate gelato—Liam and Parker were chatting about technical jargon I lost track of after the first few words. Dad and Faith were trying to pry baby names out of Becca, who was smiling but refused to divulge what they were considering, as she had when she'd been pregnant with Gracie. She liked the idea of keeping it a surprise until the baby was born.

"Uh-oh," Gracie announced dramatically.

All heads turned in her direction. She stared down at the gelato that had fallen onto the front of her pink shirt, wearing the cutest look of shock on her face as she stared at her empty spoon.

"Well, we almost made it a whole meal on one outfit," Becca said as she stood up and started to unbuckle Gracie from her booster seat. "I'll get her cleaned up and changed."

While she headed to the bathroom with Gracie, Parker cleaned off the booster seat. Liam stood with his plate in his hand to take it to the kitchen, but Faith shook her head.

"Oh, no. You're our guest," she said adamantly. "You don't need to help clear the table. Morgan, why don't you take him into the living room while your father and brother help me with the dishes?"

Dad and Parker exchanged a surprised look, because my parents had a housekeeper who usually handled cleanup, but Faith was waving them along, the picture of innocent hospitality.

I knew better. My observant stepmother was trying to play matchmaker. She'd probably seen the many looks that had passed between myself and Liam during the course of the dinner, even though I'd thought we were being subtle about it.

"Okay," I said, not upset with the fact that I'd have some alone time with Liam.

We walked toward the living room, our hands

brushing in an accidental way that made my breath catch and my pulse pick up before we even crossed the doorway.

CHAPTER FIFTEEN

Liam

I WASN'T SURE how I ended up alone in the living room with Morgan, but I didn't mind. She looked gorgeous tonight, her sexy red dress outlining her breasts in a way that made my mouth water. It wasn't too revealing for a family dinner, but the hem fell to mid-thigh, allowing me to enjoy the sight of her long legs on display.

The living room was large, with a vaulted ceiling and a stone fireplace where two armchairs sat. The couch was cream-colored suede, and there was a toybox in the corner of the room that I was sure was stuffed with Gracie's toys.

Morgan moved to the large window, pulling aside the heavy blue curtain to look outside. I strolled to the fireplace, where a curved wooden mantle held a collection of framed pictures. My eyes caught on a photo of a little girl that was unmistakably Morgan. Her green eyes shone as she smiled, revealing an adorable gap in her front teeth.

In another photo, she looked a little older, but was

still young and standing next to a woman with a similar figure to the Morgan that I knew. They also had the same mahogany hair.

"Is this your mother?" I asked as she came to stand next to me.

"Yes." She picked up a different picture, one that showed her in a birthday hat while sitting in front of a cake, and both of her parents were standing behind her. The candle revealed it was her seventh birthday. "She was pretty, wasn't she?"

I didn't miss the tender nostalgia in her voice. "Yeah," I said honestly. They shared many of the same striking features that shaped Morgan's own beauty.

"She died when I was eight," she said, tracing a finger over her mom's face in the photograph, her touch reverent.

"That must have been hard."

"You have no idea." She put the picture back on the mantle. "I didn't even have a firm concept of death at that age. No one else in my life had ever died before. So, even though she was sick for a while before she went, it was tough to grasp that she was gone forever. I needed her, you know? She was my everything. I mean, I've always been close to my dad too, but it's different with a girl and her mom."

The pain in her voice made my chest tighten. Without thinking, I took her hand, grounding her as we both looked at the row of photos stretching across the mantle. Time changed frame by frame, first just her and her father, then Faith and Parker appeared, woven into their story and lives.

"There are a lot of pictures of you with Parker," I observed, nodding toward one of them riding horses together, their grins wide and carefree.

She smiled, her eyes warming as she focused on the image. "He was four years older than me, a teenager when our parents got married, and I wasn't sure if he'd want me around much, but he turned out to be the best brother ever. Right from the beginning, we were close. Even before I developed a close relationship with Faith. I think that having Parker in my life helped me to get past my mom's death more than anything else."

"I get that. My brothers are my best friends. They've been there for me through so much," I said, sharing something about myself as well since she just opened up to me so completely.

I nodded to a picture of her farther down the mantle. She was wearing a cap and gown and standing between two people. On one side, I recognized Whitney. On the other, there was a man with dimples in his cheeks, his arm slung casually around her shoulders.

"Who is that guy?" I asked her.

Her hand dropped from mine. "Just an old friend." Her tone cooled, and she moved away from the fireplace, heading for the couch and sitting down. "I have no idea why Faith still displays that picture," she muttered beneath her breath.

I followed, settling in beside her, curious about the

sudden shift in her demeanor and the hint of annoyance I'd detected in her tone. She'd been so open about her mom, sharing those emotional memories without hesitation. This evasiveness felt…deliberate.

"What kind of old friend are we talking about here?" I pressed gently.

She sighed, leaning back against the couch cushions while her fingers fidgeted in her lap. "Trust me, he isn't worth talking about."

I smiled at Morgan, realizing I wanted to know everything about her, and the fact that she didn't want to talk about this *friend* told me there was more there than she was letting on. "Indulge me."

She met my gaze, hesitating a moment. I waited patiently, and she finally exhaled a deep breath and opened up to me. "The short story is, his name is James. I was crazy about him in college. I thought I loved him, but he didn't feel the same." Her words came out measured, but a shadow of old hurt clouded her expression.

"What happened?" I asked, sensing there was more.

A faint, wry smile pulled at her lips, though it didn't reach her eyes. "We spent months together. Late nights studying, long conversations that felt so real, and shared the kind of intimacy that made me believe it meant something." Her cheeks flushed slightly, but she pushed on. "I fell hard for him. He told me he wasn't looking for anything serious, but I thought if I waited long enough…well, it never happened. I was nothing more than an easy hookup for him. He broke things off right after graduation, then met someone else. Fell in love with her in weeks. Suddenly, he was ready for serious. Just not…with me."

The pain I heard in her voice made my gut clench. "Morgan—"

She shook her head and cut me off. "It's okay. I'm over him, but the whole situation…it just made me cautious with men and their motives after James. It taught me a lesson, not to chase after someone who doesn't feel the same."

Her words hung there between us, honest and unflinching, and somewhere deep in my chest guilt twisted hard as I realized just how badly my own actions had affected Morgan the night I'd left her in the hotel room. I wanted to reach out and touch her, but I could hear the rest of her family nearby and knew it wasn't the time or the place.

As I processed her words, all I could think was, *fuck, I did that to her, too.* I'd been the guy who took the connection, the intimacy, the night that meant something, and then disappeared. I hadn't meant to intentionally hurt her, but I had and now I knew just how deeply.

So many regrets hit me hard. "I'm sorry you went through that with James," I said, my voice low and laced with sincerity as I held her gaze. "And it kills me to think I might have made you feel that way, too, after the night we spent together. Leaving you the way

I did, I was dealing with my own issues, but it was wrong. I played right into those insecurities and I hate that I did."

Her expression softened, a flicker of surprise widening her eyes. "Liam—"

I shook my head, not finished yet. "I didn't leave you that night because I didn't care," I said, knowing she deserved the truth. "I left because I panicked. I hadn't dealt with my own shit yet. Not with Ivy, not with what that breakup did to me. I wasn't looking for anything real and what I felt for you in one night scared the hell out of me."

"Thank you for saying that," she whispered.

Relief eased the tightness that had gathered in my chest. "I never want to make you feel that way ever again. Like you're not enough. Because Morgan, you're *more* than enough. I know we've been taking this slow, but I need you to know that this isn't casual for me. *You're* not casual for me."

Her breath caught, her eyes went wide and bright, hope warring in their depths. "You're not casual for me, either."

The admission hung between us, honest and a little terrifying, but it shifted something profound between us, like yet another barrier crumbling. Without thinking, I leaned in, my hand lifting to cup her cheek as the promise of a kiss hung in the space between us.

Until the sound of giggles erupted from the hallway, and seconds later Gracie ran into the living room, reminding us both of where we were.

CHAPTER SIXTEEN

Morgan

THAT WAS A close call.

I quickly gathered my composure as Gracie climbed onto the couch between Liam and me, chattering away about something that had happened at preschool a few days ago. My heart was still racing, a mix of adrenaline from the almost kiss, and the emotional whirlwind of our conversation. Everything we'd revealed and shared and Liam's sincere words, *you're not casual for me.*

I could hear my dad and Parker talking as footsteps drew closer, and seconds later they walked into the living room, with Faith trailing behind with a tray of coffee, cream, and sugar.

Liam and I accepted a cup, and for the next hour we all sat around, talking about inconsequential things. I was on the couch with Gracie on my lap, while Liam had moved to sit in one of the armchairs by the fireplace right after she'd interrupted us.

Time seemed to drag on, even though the conversation was pleasant. Finally, Gracie began dozing off in my lap, and it was decided that the dinner party should end. Parker took his family home first, while Faith thanked Liam for coming, and Dad told him how much he appreciated his work at GalvaTech. It was a bit of a drawn-out goodbye, and I could've left, but I lingered so that we were leaving the house at the same time.

My car was in the driveway, and Liam had parked behind me. As we stepped off the porch, his hand took mine again, just like he did when we were in front of the fireplace, talking about my mother and the darkest times of my life.

Then, it felt like he was providing silent support in the only way he knew how. It was different as we strolled across the white rocks to my car, which was parked off to the side. His grip was loose, our fingers intertwined, and he ran the pad of his thumb over my knuckles.

It was intimate in a way that made me feel warm inside. We didn't say much, but we'd talked enough tonight.

When we reached my car, we walked around to the driver's side door where we wouldn't be seen if someone happened to look out the living room window. Liam moved in close before I could pull out my car keys. He pressed me back against the cool metal of the door, caging me in with his body like he'd finally lost the last thin thread of his restraint.

One hand slid into my hair, gripping just tight enough to make my knees buckle. The other found my hip, fingers digging in. His erection, hard and insistent, pressed against my stomach, igniting a blaze of heat in my veins that made my core clench with need.

"Liam," I breathed.

He didn't go for my lips right away. Instead, he dragged his mouth along my jawline in hot, open-mouthed kisses, then down the sensitive column of my neck, making me shiver. He sucked and nipped at the skin until a husky moan escaped me.

My hands slid inside his suit jacket. My palms splayed across the firm expanse of his chest, feeling the rapid beat of his heart, which matched mine. I ran my hands over his torso, reveling in the subtle flex of muscle as he exhaled a shaky breath against my throat. God, he smelled like spice and desire, and every brush of his lips sent sparks racing through me.

When he finally claimed my mouth, it wasn't careful or sweet. It was dominant and possessive. The kind of kiss that said *I want you, and I'm done pretending otherwise.* His tongue swept past my lips, delving in to taste me like I was his to devour. I felt utterly owned by him and it was intoxicating, a heady rush of sensation that made my thighs tremble.

I wanted more, craved him stripping me bare somewhere private, his intense focus unraveling me all night long. I moaned into his mouth and he swallowed the sound, rolling his hips against me in a slow, deliberate grind that had me arching into him.

He finally broke the kiss with a ragged groan, pressing his forehead to mine, our panting breaths mingling in the cool night air. His brown eyes looked almost black in the shadowed driveway, burning with a raw, undeniable lust.

I was done denying him and what I ached for so badly. "Should we continue this somewhere else?" I suggested, my tone breathless and teasing, though desperation edged every word.

"Your place or mine?" he growled, his relief evident in the husky timbre of his voice.

Thank God he felt it, too. "My place is closer."

Decision made, he followed me there in his car, the short drive a torturous blur of anticipation. The moment we stepped inside my apartment and the door slammed shut behind us, all the sexual tension that had been building between us for weeks exploded like a fuse reaching its final spark.

I spun toward him, crashing my lips to his in a wild, desperate kiss, our tongues tangling fiercely as we stumbled through the living room toward my bedroom. His hands were everywhere, yanking at the zipper of my dress with frantic urgency, peeling the fabric down my shoulders as I shoved his suit jacket off and let it drop to the floor.

"Fuck, Morgan," he groaned against my mouth, his voice rough with hunger as he tugged my dress lower, exposing my lace bra and the swells of my breasts.

We didn't make it far before I ripped at his shirt buttons, popping a couple in my haste to get him naked. He kicked off his shoes mid-stride, and I toed off my heels, our bodies colliding against each other in the hallway.

His mouth claimed mine harder, teeth grazing my lower lip as he backed me against the wall, one hand diving into my panties to stroke between my thighs. I gasped into the kiss, bucking against his fingers, my pussy already soaked and aching for him.

I fumbled with his belt, managing to get the front unfastened so that my hand could reach inside and palm his stiff cock. He growled, lifting me effortlessly, my legs wrapping around his waist as he carried me the rest of the way to the bedroom, our kisses turning deep and feverish. We tumbled onto the bed in a tangle of limbs, him kicking his pants free while I shimmied out of my dress and bra and panties, baring myself completely. He shed his boxers, his cock springing free—hard, thick, and ready—before he pounced, pinning me beneath him.

Above me, his gaze met mine as he hesitated, a pained look on his face. "Do I need a condom? I don't have one with me, but I swear I'm clean."

"I'm good, too. I'm also on birth control," I said, needing him desperately. "And I want you to fuck me bare."

His eyes flashed with raw, primal hunger. Our mouths fused again in a bruising kiss, tongues battling as he positioned himself between my spread thighs. I gripped his shoulders, nails digging in, urging him on. With one hard, powerful thrust, he buried himself inside me, filling me completely, the stretch of him delicious and overwhelming.

"Yes," I moaned, breaking the kiss to arch my back, my hips rising to meet his frantic rhythm.

There was nothing slow, soft, or sweet about the way he fucked me, and after weeks of so much self-control we were past our breaking point and I wouldn't have wanted it any other way. He didn't hold back, pounding into me with wild, rushed strokes, each one hitting deep and perfect.

His hands roamed possessively, one pinching my nipple while the other gripped my thigh to spread me wider as his hips snapped roughly against mine. He ravaged my neck with hot kisses and sharp, claiming love bites. I clawed at his back, lost in the frenzy, my moans mixing with his guttural growls as the bed creaked under us.

The end built fast, the tension coiling tight in my core until I shattered around him, crying out his name as waves of pleasure crashed over me. He followed seconds later, thrusting deep one last time with a ragged curse as he spilled inside me, then collapsed on top of me, our bodies trembling in the aftermath.

When we came down from the adrenaline rush of our orgasms, we lay there, panting and entwined, the wild rush giving way to a satisfied haze of pleasure. As our breaths slowed, I knew this was more than just giving in to a reckless moment of desire. It was us, finally letting ourselves want more.

It felt like the start of everything I had ever desired.

CHAPTER SEVENTEEN

Liam

INVESTING IN A new company always kept me busy, but this time of the year was another level entirely. Christmas was a few weeks away, and GalvaTech would be closed between the holidays, which meant every department was scrambling to hit deadlines before the break. Prototypes needed final revisions. Marketing assets had to be prepped. Contracts required signatures. CES prep was ramping toward full throttle for the first week in January.

And through all of it, Morgan and I barely had a minute to ourselves.

Four days had passed since dinner at her parent's house. Four days since we'd crossed that line and slept together again. It had been good. Not just the sex. *Everything.*

I'd stayed the night, wrapped around her in a way I hadn't held a woman in years, knowing I wasn't going anywhere this time. She'd fallen asleep with her cheek on my chest, her hand resting right over my heart like it belonged there. And in the morning, after a slower, lazier round of sex, we'd showered together. She made coffee while I cooked us breakfast, moving around her kitchen like we'd been doing it for years. Being together had felt so natural. So easy and comfortable.

I kissed her before leaving. Not because I was caught up in the high of the night before, and not because I couldn't help myself—though that was part of it—but because it felt like an honest and natural thing to do.

I wanted her to know that I wasn't running. Not this time.

Now, at the office and already mid-week, the last four days had been a blur of other pressing demands. I'd barely had a second alone with her. We were together constantly, but always surrounded by employees or buried in tasks. We'd brush past each other in the hallway, exchange a look loaded with too much meaning, and then have to pretend nothing had happened between us because we'd decided to keep things to ourselves for now. It was torture of the best kind.

Despite our inability to get that time alone, I made sure we texted each other throughout the day. I was determined to do things right this time around. If face-to-face conversations alone were impossible at the moment, I would take any form of communication with Morgan I could get beyond business.

Underneath all of that, a knot of worry kept tightening in my chest. It had been a long time since I'd been in a real relationship, and every time I thought about how badly my engagement had imploded, a small part of me panicked and doubts seeped in. My biggest worry was, could I do this the right way with Morgan?

When Ivy and I were together, I'd let work consume everything. My time, my energy, my attention. I'd been a man who'd worked twelve-hour days on Wall Street, would come home exhausted, and only offered crumbs of affection. I knew things weren't good between Ivy and I, and I knew toward the end I'd chosen work because it felt easier than dealing with the emotional mess I'd made of our relationship.

The truth was, I didn't want to be that man again. Not with Morgan. I needed to find a balance because she deserved someone who showed up. Fully. Consistently. Someone who chose her and made time for her.

I knew this, but I couldn't deny that there was a part of me that was terrified I'd fuck it all up again.

After normal work hours on Thursday, I unexpectedly found myself with a block of free time while Morgan was in a meeting with the marketing team before everyone left for the evening. Instead of reviewing another cost analysis spreadsheet, I decided to take the time to place a call to one of the most content married men I knew. My brother, Noah.

He answered on the first ring and we exchanged greetings and the usual small talk to catch up.

Finally, I said, "So, I wanted to talk to you about…being in a relationship."

There was distinct silence before Noah replied. "Is

this Liam?"

I huffed out a laugh despite myself. "Very funny. Are you going to help me out or not?"

"I guess it depends on what you want from me," he said, amusement fading into genuine curiosity.

"Just listen," I said, and launched into the story of Morgan and me.

I started with the night we met, skipping the intimate details and glossing over how my skepticism about marriage had driven me from his wedding reception in the first place.

"Now we've been dating, or whatever this is, for a few weeks, but I'm slammed at the office, exhausted from the grind here and jumping in to help Simon with the angel investment firm whenever he needs it. I haven't spent any quality time with her, and I can't shake the feeling that I'm already screwing this up."

Noah remained quiet while I talked. He was a good listener, which was another reason he was the person I chose to call.

"I'm struggling to see the problem here," he said when I finished. "It sounds like you both have demanding schedules right now. That's not a relationship crisis. That's life."

I rose from my desk and paced to the window, pressing the phone tighter to my ear, the city lights blurring below. "She's the first woman I've tried to be serious about since Ivy. I keep worrying I'll repeat the same mistakes with Morgan that I did with her."

"Liam," Noah said in that brotherly tone of his.

"You're not in that place anymore, and Morgan isn't Ivy."

I rubbed a hand along the back of my neck. "I know that."

"I remember how much you worked when you were with Ivy," Noah said, without judgment. "But this? It sounds like it's a busy period at the company that will blow over after the New Year. You're overthinking everything because the relationship is new. Give it time. If this is someone you truly want in your life, you'll find a way to make it work."

"Time," I said, hearing the doubt in my own voice. "What if I don't have time? What if—"

"You're catastrophizing," Noah said bluntly. "Do you really think Morgan is going to cheat on you the way Ivy did?"

The question hit like a punch to the gut, but my answer was immediate. "No." Ivy had been unhappy for years, and there had been a lack of communication between us I was determined not to repeat with Morgan.

"Then what are you afraid of?" Noah asked.

I exhaled slowly. "That I'll lose her anyway. That I'll be so focused on work that I'll lose sight of what's important. That she'll realize she deserves better and walk away or find someone else who—"

"Liam." Noah's voice turned firm. "Ivy cheated because of Ivy. Not because you worked too much or didn't pay attention or whatever bullshit excuse she gave you. She made a choice. And yeah, maybe you did work too much, but that doesn't change the fact that she betrayed you."

"I know that—"

"Do you? Because it sounds like you're blaming yourself for her wandering eye and trying to make yourself the villain in this new story before it's even begun."

Just talking to Noah helped ease my anxieties. "Marriage has made you wise," I quipped, a reluctant smile tugging at my lips.

He laughed. "I've always been wise, but you're not one to ask for advice. Reaching out like this? It tells me this woman means something to you."

"She does," I admitted quietly, my chest tightening with the admission. "I never thought I'd try to make a serious relationship work again. She's special and I care about her. More than I expected."

"So stop panicking and anticipating the worst," Noah said. "Build this relationship. Don't run from it."

A sound behind me made me turn around, and I nearly dropped the phone when I saw Morgan standing there with a white plastic bag in her hand.

"I've got to go, Noah. I'll call you back later," I muttered, ending the call abruptly, my face heating as I wondered how much she'd overheard.

She held up the white take-out bag with a small, tentative smile. "I wasn't sure how late you planned to stay tonight, but everyone else is gone and I thought that maybe we could squeeze in a quick dinner together. Well, everyone but Parker, but he's holed up in his office with the door shut, which means he's engrossed in something he deems important and doesn't want to be disturbed."

I cleared my throat. "Dinner sounds great."

Embarrassment prickled at my neck, still unsure how much she'd overheard of me confiding in my brother about my insecurities. I moved toward the small sitting area, trying to play it cool, but before I reached it, Morgan turned back to the door, shutting it firmly and twisting the lock with a deliberate click.

She set the bag on one of the chairs in front of my desk then sauntered toward me with that slow, confident sway that turned my brain to static. Her gaze locked on mine, and a seductive smile curved her lips.

"I care about you too, Liam," she said, grabbing my tie and pulling me in for a kiss.

Heat flooded through me instantly. I cupped her face, deepening the kiss, pouring everything I was worried about, everything I'd just confessed to Noah, into the way my mouth moved against hers.

When she pulled back, her eyes were bright, her lips swollen. "You're not screwing this up," she whispered.

"You heard that?" My voice came out rough.

She nodded, but didn't let go of my tie, keeping me tethered to her, which I didn't mind. "And for the record? I know you're busy. I'm busy, too. But that doesn't mean I think you don't care. We'll figure it out."

The knot in my chest loosened. "You make it sound simple."

"Maybe it is." She smiled. "Maybe we're both overthinking this because it matters. Because we don't want to mess it up."

"I don't want to mess this up," I reiterated quietly.

"Then don't." she kissed me again, softer this time. "Show up when you can. Communicate when you can't. Trust that I'm not going anywhere just because we're both working hard right now."

Trust. The word hung between us, and I pulled her closer, kissing her again, but this time making sure I did so with enough heat that I stopped questioning what was happening between us. My cock hardened painfully in my pants, straining against the fabric as I crushed her body to mine, reveling in the lush press of her curves. She released my tie, looping her arms around my neck, and I deepened the kiss, my tongue delving in to taste her sweetness, my hips grinding forward instinctively, seeking the friction that made my blood roar.

The world shrank to just us. The electric contact of our bodies, the lust crackling like wildfire. I lost myself in her, my hands roaming her back, pulling her tighter to me as need pulsed hot and urgent between us.

When she pulled away, I chased her lips with a low growl, but she planted a hand on my chest, her eyes soft and reassuring. "I'm not going anywhere just because we've both been busy lately."

Her tone was gentle, easing the knot of vulnerability in my chest right before a mischievous glint sparked in her eyes and her hands dropped to the front of my pants. I shuddered as her palm brushed my throbbing erection, sending jolts of pleasure straight through my dick.

"We'll just have to find ways to reconnect when we can," she purred, her voice laced with wicked intent as she began unbuckling my belt, then unfastening the front of my slacks, tugging them down my hips until my dick sprang free. "Like here, and now, and like this."

She backed me up a step, until my backside was braced against one of the armchairs, then she dropped to her knees, her intent clear. Her fingers wrapped around my cock, stroking from base to tip. She licked her lips, her eyes looking up at me with a sultry promise.

Without thinking, I reached out, my fingers threading through her silky hair, my cock already leaking. "Baby, you don't have to—"

The words faded away as she leaned in, her lips parting to take the head of my cock into her warm, wet mouth. Electric pleasure shot through me, and I bit back a groan, struggling to keep quiet as bolts of ecstasy lit up every nerve ending.

"Morgan…" I buried my fingers harder into her hair, gripping the strands to anchor myself as she took me deeper, her mouth sliding down until I hit the back of her throat. She retreated slowly, swirling her tongue around the sensitive head, teasing with expert flicks that made my knees weak.

"Fuck. Don't tease me," I rasped, my voice roughening with desperation.

Her hand gripped the base, pumping in rhythm as she bobbed her head, sucking with perfect pressure—wet, hot, relentless. Her tongue laved the underside of my dick, her cheeks hollowing with each pull. It was heaven, and I barreled toward the edge faster than ever. My body thrummed with need, every swirl and suck pushing me to the brink.

"I'm close," I warned through gritted teeth, giving her an out if she wanted it. "I'm going to come, baby."

Instead she took me deeper, shattering my restraint. My head fell back, eyes squeezing shut as I basked in the bliss. I exhaled roughly, my orgasm crashing over me in waves as I came, hot and thick, down her throat. She swallowed every drop, drawing out the ecstasy until my legs were trembling and I fought to stifle the moan clawing its way up my chest. The last thing we needed was Parker overhearing us. This moment was ours alone.

Morgan released me, licking her swollen lips in a way that made my spent cock twitch and start to grow hard again. Fuck, she was going to be the death of me.

I hauled her to her feet, my hands urgent as I backed her against the edge of my desk, perching her ass on the surface. The deep purple dress she'd worn today clung to her curves like sin, but I shoved the skirt up to her waist, exposing black lacy panties that made my mouth go dry and my pulse race.

"I hoped you'd get a chance to see them," she said, her voice husky with desire, eyes dark and inviting. "I wore them for you."

"Are you wet for me?" I growled, my tone rough with renewed desire. "Did sucking me off turn you on?"

I didn't wait for an answer. I pushed my hand into her panties to feel her slick heat for myself. She was drenched, swollen, ready. Morgan whimpered, the sound needy and muffled as I captured her mouth in a searing kiss, my tongue plunging deep while I slid two fingers inside her tight warmth. She arched against my hand, her breasts pressing into my chest, her fingers gripping my biceps like a lifeline, nails digging in as if fearing I'd stop.

Not a chance. I needed to watch her unravel, to feel her come undone under my touch.

My lips trailed along her jaw, nipping her earlobe sharply enough to make her jerk and gasp. Her breathy moans filled my ear as I pumped my fingers in and out, then curled them to hit that perfect spot inside her, while my thumb circled her clit with firm pressure.

"Oh, God," she whispered, her voice a breathless plea that made this forbidden encounter even hotter. "Liam…it feels so good."

I angled my hand to grind my palm against her sensitive clit while dragging my tongue up the side of her neck, tasting her skin. She gasped, her legs quivering around me, inner walls clenching tighter.

"Don't stop," she begged, her words fractured

with need. "Liam…"

I'd never tire of hearing my name on her lips like that. Desperate and reverent. I quickened my pace, thrusting faster, deeper, pulling back just enough to watch her flushed face as her ecstasy built. Her lips parted, lashes fluttering shut as she shattered, her body convulsing around my fingers in rhythmic pulses. A stifled cry of pleasure escaped her as she came hard, soaking my hand.

She was beautiful. So utterly fucking beautiful.

I withdrew my fingers slowly, bringing them to my mouth to lick them clean, savoring her taste while her dark eyes watched and flared with heat. That intimate look alone reassured me, chasing away my fears of distance creeping in and ruining what we were building before we even had the chance to figure out who we could become.

My past wasn't my present. Morgan was different and so was I.

And finally, I felt ready to leave it all behind, where it belonged.

CHAPTER EIGHTEEN
Morgan

THE MALL WAS packed with shoppers, as was typical this time of year. With Christmas just around the corner, there were plenty of people trying to finish buying gifts for everyone on their lists. That was exactly why I was here with Becca.

"Are you sure that Parker will like this?" I asked, holding up a package of *Star Wars* socks. "I'm worried that socks are a lame gift."

"Those aren't just any socks," Becca said with an indulgent smile, as if I just didn't get it. To be fair, I didn't. "Those are *Star Wars* socks. Anything with pictures of Yoda or Darth Vadar is a good gift for him."

I laughed and shook my head. "He's such a nerd."

"And that's one of the many reasons we adore him."

I couldn't argue with that. I'd always found his nerdiness endearing.

We headed to the register, and I bought Parker's socks while Becca purchased a ladybug nightlight for

Gracie and a new tie for my dad.

After that, we strolled through the mall, passing clothing stores and a smoothie shop before we went into a toy store. This was the most crowded store we'd been to, and it was hard to walk around without bumping into someone.

"You'll have to help me choose something for Gracie," I said, scanning the store for that perfect gift for my niece. "I want to make sure she loves whatever I get her. She deserves a great Christmas since she'll be sharing the attention with her little brother next year."

My eyes were on a display of baby dolls as I spoke but when Becca didn't reply immediately, I glanced at her. To my surprise, she was frowning.

"What's wrong?" I asked, my eyes immediately going to her stomach. "Is it the baby?"

She waved off my concern. "No, not at all. It's just…what you said. I had the same thought. I wanted to go a little big this year for Gracie because as excited as she is to become a big sister, this is going to be a huge change for her. She's used to being the only child and getting all the attention."

"Makes sense," I said, nodding thoughtfully. "A little spoiling sometimes isn't a bad thing."

"But Parker disagrees," Becca continued, her frown deepening as she absently toyed with a stuffed unicorn on a shelf. "He told me that he didn't think we should go too overboard on gifts for her."

That didn't sound right to me. Parker adored Gracie, and he was the first person I'd expect to want to give her an especially magical Christmas.

"It's not just that," Becca added, her voice dropping as we meandered deeper into the store. "He's also cancelled our babymoon trip."

"Your what?" I asked, confused by the term.

She sighed. "It's a little vacation that a couple takes together before the baby is born. A last chance to get some quality time in before you're overwhelmed with diapers and sleepless nights," she explained, her disappointment evident in the slight slump of her shoulders. "I didn't know about them before Gracie was born, but now that I do, I really wanted the two of us to do this. I'd planned it during New Year's, but all of a sudden, Parker is worried about travelling while I'm pregnant, even though my doctor said it would be perfectly safe."

I could see that she was frustrated, but I didn't know what to say to make her feel better. Parker wasn't usually this overprotective of Becca. Combined with his take on how to handle Gracie's Christmas gifts, along with some over the top reactions about a few things at work, including the increase to the marketing budget, his behavior had been strange lately.

"Maybe he's just feeling pressure about the upcoming launch," I said as my eyes skimmed over some board games. "He did seem rather stressed during last week's meeting."

She sighed. "This new EV charger and making it a success is important to him. I get that, but I'm also disappointed."

"How about you guys plan a nice date night instead?" I suggested, aiming to lift her spirits. "Do something fun. Maybe dinner and a show along with one night at a hotel. Christmastime in New York City is beautiful. I'll watch Gracie."

Becca gave me a smile that didn't quite reach her eyes. "Maybe. Thanks, Morgan."

She helped me pick out gifts for Gracie—a Disney princess coloring book, new crayons, and a matching doll—and we left the store. My mind lingered on Parker, wondering what was really going on with him, but Becca didn't seem to want to discuss it any further.

"So, how are things going with Liam?" she asked as we walked past a kiosk where a man selling expensive sunglasses tried to get our attention. I gave him my best polite but uninterested smile and we continued on.

I'd confided in Becca about Liam, and how we were quietly dating. "Things are mostly good," I said, feeling my cheeks heat as I thought about our steamy encounter in his office a couple of days ago.

I hadn't planned to initiate anything sexual when I showed up at his office with dinner, but after I overheard his phone conversation and realized he was worried about screwing things up with me, it had prompted me to act boldly. I had no regrets, though I never imagined doing something like that at work. But I couldn't deny our secrecy made the whole thing even more thrilling and exhilarating. The need to be quiet, the forbidden nature of what we were doing…

"Mostly good?" Becca pressed, her brow arching with curiosity. "What does that mean?"

I shrugged. "We've both been swamped at work lately," I said, trying to sound casual. "I love that the company shuts down for the holidays to give everyone a chance to enjoy that time off, but this is always a busy time in preparation of that. We just haven't had much time alone. But we text every day, and he's…" I paused, searching for the right word. "Sweet."

That last part was only partially true. Liam *could* be surprisingly sweet, sure, but our recent messages leaned more toward the explicit, and I flushed just thinking about them. Like this morning's text where he'd described in vivid detail what he'd been thinking about while in the shower.

My blush intensified, and Becca's knowing smile told me she'd noticed. The gleam in her eyes confirmed it.

"Uh, huh. I'm sure those texts are sweet and completely innocent." She suddenly grabbed my arm and steered me toward a lingerie store. "Come on. Let's stop in here and find something to make his jaw drop."

"Oh, I don't know about that." But I was already thinking about Liam's reaction to my simple black lace underwear in his office. What would he do if I wore something even more daring?

"Parker mentioned you and Liam are heading to Vegas in January for CES." Becca's grin turned mischievous as she pulled me through the store's doors. "He suspects nothing, but I'm guessing that it won't be an entirely business focused trip for you and Liam."

"We haven't actually discussed it—"

"Talking is overrated," Becca said with a laugh, her mood uplifted. "You two will be alone in a hotel in *Sin City*. Trust me, you'll want sexy lingerie to make it unforgettable."

I bit my bottom lip and glanced around at the displays, taking in the array of bras, panties, camisoles, bodysuits, and even silky robes. A thrill of anticipation shot through me. Becca was right. Vegas promised the perfect opportunity to deepen the connection with Liam, especially if I wore something from this store to tempt him.

Our trip to Sin City was definitely going to be one to remember.

CHAPTER NINETEEN

Liam

WHILE GALVATECH CLOSED over the holidays, the investment firm didn't. So, while the employees of GalvaTech, including Morgan, took the week off to spend time with their families, I'd been busy with Simon at our own business, hammering out details of upcoming deals and catching up on end of the year assessments, internal audits, and client updates.

Even with all the extra hours I was putting in, this schedule wasn't nearly as relentless as my Wall Street days. Back then, work consumed every waking moment. This was just a temporary crunch. A couple of demanding weeks I knew would pass.

Still, frustration gnawed at me. I hadn't managed any real time alone with Morgan. We talked mostly business at work, traded texts that ranged from sweet to filthy, but we hadn't been alone together since that evening in my office over two weeks ago.

Christmas came and went, as did New Year's Eve. Because we hadn't made the fact that we were dating public yet, we decided to spend the holidays separately. But I knew at some point we'd have to face the truth. What we were building was something real, and I needed to figure out a way to let Parker and her father know that I was fully invested in Morgan and our developing relationship, without rocking the boat professionally.

For now, I couldn't wait to get her alone in Vegas. The office was back in full swing after the holidays, and we were leaving tomorrow.

"I've finalized our travel arrangements," Morgan said, standing in my office.

Unfortunately, her father was at her side, so there was zero chance of spreading her out on my desk and fucking her the way I'd been fantasizing about after not seeing her for the past week.

"This is exciting," Samuel said, giving his daughter's shoulder an affectionate squeeze. "With this being the first time GalvaTech has attended the Consumer Electronics Show, I can only imagine the level of exposure we will receive."

I smiled at his enthusiasm. "It's definitely the beginning of a new chapter for the company." I checked the time on my phone before lifting my gaze back to Morgan. "I'm heading out for the day. Simon asked me to meet with him this afternoon, but I'll see you at the airport tomorrow."

Her smile and nod were nothing but professional, but her gaze simmered with the same eager anticipation I was feeling about having some quality time to ourselves in Vegas.

I left GalvaTech, and as I walked into our firm, Simon's newest assistant glared at me from behind her desk, frazzled and visibly irritated. I greeted her, and she muttered something beneath her breath I didn't quite catch, but I knew was not complimentary toward my brother. At this rate, Simon was going to burn through every qualified candidate in the city and would have to function without help entirely.

The door to Simon's office was open, so I strolled in to find him frowning at his computer screen. He looked up when he heard my footsteps, and a muscle in his jaw ticked.

"Is another one about to bite the dust?" I asked, jerking my thumb toward the door behind me.

"What are you talking about?" he asked, completely oblivious to the very unhappy woman outside his office.

"Your latest assistant," I said, dropping into one of the chairs in front of his desk. "She looks like she's about to quit and key your car on the way out."

"She's fine," he scoffed.

"She not fine," I countered. "She looked at me like you were personally responsible for ruining her life. What did you do this time?"

"*I* didn't do anything," he said defensively. "She double booked me for two separate meetings this morning, then forwarded an internal email chain, *with my notes*, to the actual client. Every damn comment. Including the one where I said his proposal 'needed divine intervention'."

I had to swallow back my laughter, because I knew this was serious stuff for Simon. I also knew he'd probably driven the poor woman to the brink with all his demands and she hadn't been thinking straight.

"She's been here two weeks," he went on, scrubbing a hand over his face like the weight of her incompetence physically pained him. "She should be able to handle basic tasks by now."

I arched a brow. "It's not easy when you're barking orders without so much as a 'please' or 'thank you'."

"I don't have time for pleasantries," he said, his tone annoyed. "This is business, not a social club."

I huffed out a quiet breath. I'd heard this argument from him enough times to know logic wasn't going to get through to him. "It's also not a revolving door, but you've gone through, what, three assistants already in the last six months?"

"Four," he corrected without a hint of shame. "And the common denominator isn't me. It's their inability to keep up. But we have bigger problems right now. We need to talk."

The abrupt change in his tone, from irritated to concern, caught my attention. "Why do I suddenly have a bad feeling about whatever this problem is?"

He turned his laptop around and pushed it forward so that I could see what was on the screen. I scanned the most recent profit and loss statement from GalvaTech. I'd already reviewed the report yesterday when it hit my own inbox, and everything seemed fine to me.

I glanced up at him, unsure what the issue was. "Okay, what am I missing?"

"Look closer," Simon said, his tone insistent. "It's subtle."

This was Simon's specialty. I was decent with numbers, but my strength was in business management and working directly with the companies we invested in. Simon, however, excelled at dissecting financials, and his keen eye had saved us from bad investments more than once.

So, I leaned in, scrutinizing the figures and finally saw the subtle decline in capital. He was right. Something was off.

I glanced back at him. "The money we invested is going out fast," I said.

"Way too fast," Simon agreed, reclaiming the laptop. "Based on the projected budget and allocation of funds to each department we'd forecasted, it doesn't add up."

I dragged a hand through my hair. "At this rate, our investment will be gone well before the launch even happens. But is this legitimate? Could it just be expenses in areas we hadn't anticipated?"

"The red flag for me is definitely the operating expenses, which seem inflated based on the breakdown of monthly costs we were given," Simon said, a frown pulling down his brows. "Something isn't right. I want to hire a forensic accountant to look over all the financial records so we have a clearer picture of what's draining the capital so quickly."

"Agreed," I said without hesitation, because our firm would be the one taking the biggest hit on any financial mismanagement at GalvaTech.

Simon hesitated. He wasn't one to hold back speaking his mind, so this uncharacteristic pause made me a little uneasy.

"I think we need to keep this between the two of us for now," he said carefully. "No one at GalvaTech should know we're looking into this. Including Morgan."

His gaze was direct and knowing. I'd told Simon about my one night with Morgan, but the fact that he'd singled her out now told me he was somehow aware of my current non-business relationship with her, which I hadn't mentioned to him.

"You know about me and Morgan?" I asked cautiously.

He leaned back in his chair. "Remember when you forgot your phone in the conference room when you were in the office last week, when you went to grab us dinner from the deli down the street? She texted you four times while you were gone."

I glared at him. "You looked at my phone?"

"I wasn't snooping," he said, sounding offended I'd even think such a thing. "It kept going off and distracting me while I was trying to review the proposal from that health food company we've been considering. I just glanced over and saw her name on the screen multiple times, and I may or may not have seen part of her texts to you."

I expected judgement from Simon, but his expression remained neutral. But if I recalled correctly, those messages she'd sent while I'd been out grabbing dinner had been…sexy enough to be incriminating.

"Okay, fine," I admitted. "I'm seeing her. But it's not affecting the job."

"Then you won't have a problem keeping this from her." He held my gaze. "*None* of the Starlings need to know about our concerns until we have some definitive answers."

Every muscle in my body tensed. "Morgan has nothing to do with this."

I didn't know what the hell was going on, but I knew with absolute certainty that she'd never compromise the integrity of her family's company.

"That might be the case," Simon conceded, his voice firm but not accusatory. "But it doesn't change anything. We need to wait until the forensic consultant's results come in before we tell *anyone.*"

I clenched my jaw, hating the idea of keeping secrets from her. But I understood Simon's logic, which was frustratingly valid. If someone was embezzling, which seemed to be a strong possibility, it could be someone Morgan knew. Someone she trusted or cared about. Telling her now would be more of a burden on her, because it would be a secret she'd have to keep from everyone, including her family. It was better that she didn't know. At least for now.

"Fine," I said, though my reluctance was clear. "I'll keep this quiet, but this becomes our top priority. I want answers on where the money is going as soon as possible."

Until then, I'd have to keep Morgan in the dark. For her own good. Even if it went against every grain in my body to keep something this important from her.

CHAPTER TWENTY

Morgan

THE FLIGHT FROM New York to Las Vegas took six hours, and I spent the entire time wishing I'd booked Liam's seat beside mine. I'd had full control over the flight arrangements but I'd gotten too caught up in worrying about the optics of it all. Would Jenny and Carlos, the two salespeople accompanying us, suspect something was going on? Would my dad think it strange if he saw the travel information filed with the accounting department? Most importantly, would we be able to keep our hands off each other if we were sitting so close for so long?

About an hour into the flight, while Jenny launched into a passionate conversation about the fish in her saltwater tank, I realized I'd made a terrible decision. She was one of my best salespeople and a genuinely sweet person, but she wasn't Liam. Meanwhile, he and Carlos were seated directly behind us.

My overthinking and worrying too much cost me six hours next to the man I was getting desperate to spend some alone time with.

Luckily, Liam didn't have the same problem. He'd insisted on handling the hotel reservations himself, and when we arrived, I discovered why. He'd made sure we had adjoining rooms.

Any concern about how that might look evaporated the moment we stepped off the elevator on our floor and walked down the hallway side by side. He gave me a quick, private smile full of promise as we unlocked our doors to our suites. I hadn't even made it a few steps inside when I heard the unmistakable sound of him unlocking his side of the doors separating our rooms.

Feeling a little giddy, I did the same. Unfortunately, there was no time to take advantage of our close proximity. With the three-hour time change putting us in Vegas early in the morning, we had just enough of a window to drop our things off before heading straight to the convention center for CES.

Jenny and Carlos were already waiting for us in the lobby when we came back downstairs, and the next several hours into the early evening were filled with work, but it was one of the most exciting business experiences I'd ever had. With our booth already set up, we took our place among bigwigs in the tech industry showcasing their own innovative products.

That first day was also Media Preview Day, where national outlets, analysts, and content creators were granted early access to product announcements and major press conferences. It was a whirlwind of activity, and we spent the afternoon talking to reporters and other company representatives in our industry. For the first time, it felt like we were really carving out a place for ourselves in the tech world.

By the time the show closed for the day, we were all exhausted. Between the travel and nonstop socializing, my whole body ached and my feet were sore from standing all day. I wanted nothing more than to just curl up on a couch and relax.

Liam and I didn't make plans, but I hoped he didn't expect too much from me this evening. As much as I wanted to be intimate with him again, I was painfully aware that my energy level was nearly depleted. Sex tonight felt questionable at best.

As soon as I reached my room, I stripped out of my clothes and took a long, hot shower, letting the water soothe my sore muscles. I assumed Liam was doing the same. I'd brought my new lingerie with me, but in that moment comfort won out, so I pulled on some plain cotton panties instead. Braless, I threw on my pajamas—a tank top with a cat wearing sunglasses on the front, and a pair of pink cotton sleep shorts.

I'd just settled on the couch in the sitting area of my hotel room when there was a knock. Not from the entrance to my room, but from the door connecting mine to Liam's.

"Come in," I called out.

The door opened and Liam stepped through carrying a pizza box, his hair still damp from his own shower. He'd changed into a pair of gray sweatpants and a fitted t-shirt that did absolutely nothing to hide the muscles underneath.

My mouth watered, and not just from the smell of pizza.

"Where did that come from?" I asked curiously, because it certainly didn't look like something on the room service menu.

"You didn't see the pizza place across the street?" He walked over to me and set the box on the table in front of the couch, along with paper plates and napkins. "I ordered before I showered. They just delivered it."

My stomach rumbled loudly in response. We'd been too busy at the show to grab a bite to eat, and it was well past dinnertime now. "Please tell me there's pepperoni on that pizza."

"Of course there is." He flipped the box open, revealing a perfect pepperoni pizza with steam still rising from the cheese.

I didn't hesitate to grab a slice, the first bite making me groan in appreciation.

Liam settled onto the couch beside me and picked up the remote. "Should we watch a movie? I'm sure we can find something on pay-per-view."

"No porn," I said around my mouthful of pizza.

He chuckled, his eyes dancing with amusement. "Not exactly what I had in mind tonight." He scrolled through our options. "Would you prefer an action flick or romantic comedy?"

"Action," I said, glancing at him from the corner of my eye, curiosity getting the better of me. "So, what are we doing here? Like, is this a laid-back date situation?"

He paused mid-scroll, turning to look at me with an easy smile. "This is just us hanging out. But I do plan on taking you on a real date tomorrow night." He picked up his own slice of pizza. "I know we're both exhausted, so tonight is just about relaxing and taking it easy."

Warmth spread through me. I hadn't expected him to arrange anything at all, let alone an actual date. "You didn't have to plan something—"

"I wanted to." His voice was firm, but gentle. "You deserve more than just adjoining hotel rooms and a secretive hookup, Morgan. I want to do things right this time."

The sincerity in his eyes made my breath catch. This man, the same one who'd walked away from me a few months ago, was actively trying. Planning. Making an effort to show me I mattered.

"Okay," I said softly, unable to stop my smile. "I'd like that."

"Good." He turned back to the TV, scrolling until he found a movie. "How about this one? Cops, car chases, and gratuitous explosions?"

I laughed. "Perfect."

After finishing my dinner, I settled back against the couch cushions, tucking my legs underneath me as the opening credits rolled. The movie was exactly what he'd promised, all explosions and shootouts with paper-thin character development, but I enjoyed it anyway.

The best part came about halfway through, when

Liam reached over and gently pulled my feet onto his lap.

"What are you—*oh*." The word turned into a low moan as he pressed his thumbs into the arch of my foot, finding that sore, aching spot from hours of standing in heels.

"Feel good?" he asked, his voice a low murmur.

I nodded, his strong hands working magic on my tired muscles.

"You were incredible today, by the way," he said, both of us only half watching the movie. "The way you handled that reporter from TechSphere was impressive."

"I was nervous the whole time." I let my head fall back against the couch cushion, my eyes drifting closed. "I kept thinking I'd say something ridiculous and it would end up in print."

"You didn't though," he said, his voice warm with praise. "You were confident. Professional. Sexy as hell in that business suit and skirt that had me staring at your ass way too often."

My eyes opened, finding him watching me instead of the TV. The movie's blue light flickered across his face, catching in his dark eyes.

"That pencil skirt was not the best choice for a long day," I admitted.

"Still distracting as hell, in the best ways." His thumb circled a particularly tender spot on the ball of my foot, making me groan softly in response. "Though I have to say, I'm partial to this look, too."

I glanced down at my well-worn, cat-wearing-sunglasses tank top and shorts. "Really? This does it for you?"

"Everything about you does it for me." The words were casual, but the heat in his gaze was anything but. "But yeah. You comfortable and relaxed, letting me take care of you? That's…" He trailed off, his jaw tightening slightly.

"That's what?" I prompted, the movie forgotten for now.

"That's something I never thought I'd want this badly." He switched to my other foot, his touch gentler now. "I've spent so long avoiding anything that felt too serious and domestic, but seeing you curled up on this couch in your pajamas, the two of us just connecting like this—simple, real, no pretenses—it's perfect."

My heart did a slow roll in my chest. "Really?"

"Really," he said, and then a sinful look glimmered in his eyes. "And as much as I want you and have imagined fucking you a dozen different ways since that evening in my office, I promise I have no expectations for tonight beyond exactly this."

I laughed softly. "What if *I* have expectations?" I teased.

"Then you can keep them for tomorrow." He pressed his thumb firmly into my arch. "After our date. After I've wined and dined you properly."

I studied Liam for a long moment, this man who kept surprising me, who was trying so hard to do things differently this time. Who wanted more than just the physical, even when we were alone in a hotel room with every opportunity to take advantage of the moment.

We fell into a comfortable silence, his hands still working their magic on my feet while car chases and gunfights played out on the TV screen. And as the exhaustion finally started pulling me under, one thought remained.

This—us together without any expectations—felt right. Tomorrow we'd have our date. But tonight, this effortless connection was more than enough.

CHAPTER TWENTY-ONE

Liam

I'D BEEN TO Las Vegas several times, but despite the city's well-known reputation for sinful indulgences, my trips always revolved around business. Conventions, trade shows, and meetings with important people. This evening, after CES, I was taking Morgan on our first official date.

I wanted our night together to be special and memorable, something beyond taking her to dinner and a show. A quick online search pointed me to the Venetian, a luxurious hotel-casino that transported guests straight to Italy with its Venice-inspired décor. As we walked hand in hand along the cobblestone path beside the indoor Grand Canal, I pointed out the gondolas drifting through the water.

"That's why we're here," I said, watching her face light up with delight.

"Really?" Her eyes went wide. "We can ride in one?"

"Yep. Come on." I led her toward the dock where the gondola I'd reserved was waiting.

I helped her into the boat, then sat beside her. Our gondolier—dressed in a striped shirt, straw hat, and a red sash that matched the cushioned seats—greeted us in an Italian accent that was either authentic or a convincing performance. When the gondola pushed off, I slid my arm around Morgan's shoulders, pulling her gently against my side.

As we floated beneath arched bridges and past storefronts designed to mimic Venetian streets, the gondolier sang in a deep baritone. The painted sky overhead gave the illusion of dusk and our thirty minute ride passed in a comfortable silence while I watched her enjoy the experience. Romance had never been my forte, but I had to admit that this hit the mark. Morgan's happy smile and the sweet kiss she gave me at the end of the ride stayed with me long after we stepped back onto the walkway.

Afterward, we dined on pasta for dinner then meandered through a mix of stores at The Venetian, mostly window-shopping without the intent to buy. All the while, I kept an eye out for any signs that there was something Morgan might like to purchase, but she didn't seem particularly drawn to anything in any of the Grand Canal Shoppes, even the high-end luxury fashion stores.

Then, we hit the bookstore and her whole demeanor changed.

It was one of those rare bookshops that smelled like leather and aged paper and focused mostly on classics and hard to find novels. The place was quiet, with only the light jingle of a bell above the door and the low murmur of conversation among the customers already present.

When we walked inside, for the first time that evening Morgan pulled away from me. She moved with quiet reverence along the shelves and I watched her trace the spines of antique volumes—some pristine, others so weathered their titles had faded. She occasionally paused to gingerly extract one, leaf through its pages, and replace it back on the shelf with care.

I pretended to browse, but mostly I watched her, utterly captivated by her beauty and the simplicity of just being with her. The more time we spent together, the deeper she drew me in. And now that it was just the two of us alone, I didn't have to hide my admiring stares.

"Oh, wow," she breathed, halting at a glass display case near the front counter.

Inside were several classics, but the one she gravitated toward was a first edition of *The Wonderful Wizard of Oz,* with a price tag of eight thousand dollars.

"It's illustrated," she said with a smile. "I bet it's beautiful."

"Should I call the woman over to open the case?" I asked.

She shook her head. "No, don't waste her time. It's lovely but expensive. More than I'm willing to spend."

Maybe so, but her gaze lingered on the book just

long enough to tell me everything I needed to know. When she excused herself to use the restroom, I didn't hesitate. I waved the shopkeeper over, asked her to unlock the case, and waited while she wrapped the book carefully in brown tissue paper. The moment she handed it to me I knew I'd made the right call. I paid and stepped toward the entrance to wait for Morgan.

Her eyes went straight to the package in my hands the second she reappeared. "What did you buy?" she asked, but the widening of her eyes told me she already knew.

I held the book out to her. "I think you're right. The illustrations are probably beautiful. You'll have to let me know."

Her hand trembled slightly as she accepted the gift, her fingers brushing over the wrapping reverently. "You didn't have to do that."

"I know," I said, sliding an arm around her waist and guiding her out of the bookstore. "But I wanted you to have something special to remember our time together here."

She still thought it was too expensive. I could see the argument forming behind her eyes, but the slow, stunned smile spreading across her face shut it down before it began. Which made the purchase worth every dime.

We strolled on, and remembering how much Morgan liked chocolate, I guided her into a specialty chocolatier shoppe next. The first thing she noticed was a chocolate fountain in a glass case. White, milk, and dark chocolate flowed from the ceiling, cascading over glass basins in a stunning display of sweet perfection. Even I had to admit it was mesmerizing, and when Morgan licked her lips, I couldn't help but laugh.

"Hungry for something sweet, baby?" I murmured, keeping my voice low so only she could hear.

Her gaze remained transfixed on the fountain. "It looks delicious."

I leaned in closer. "You know, they sell jars of that chocolate sauce." I gestured toward the counter where the glass containers lined the shelves. "Which might come in handy later on."

"Oh, yeah?" She met my gaze, her cheeks flushed a soft pink. "For what, exactly?"

"I can think of a few uses." I splayed my hand at the small of her back and didn't miss the way she shivered. "Dripping it all over you. Licking it off and taking my time doing so."

I heard her breath hitch. "Liam," she whispered, glancing around at the other customers browsing the shop, who weren't paying us any attention. "We're in public."

"I know." I grinned, enjoying the way her pupils dilated with desire. "Which is why we should probably wrap this up and head back to the hotel. Unless you'd rather stay here and let me describe in exact detail where I want to put that chocolate sauce."

She swallowed hard and shook her head, but there was a smile on her lips. "You're killing me."

"Not yet, but soon." I brushed a chaste kiss against

her temple, though my words were anything but. "So, what will it be? Dark, milk, or white chocolate?"

"Milk chocolate," she managed as I steered her toward the display. "Definitely milk chocolate."

"Good choice. My favorite, too." I flashed her a wicked grin as I picked up a jar.

"Do we need spoons?" she asked, indicating the plastic utensils the shop offered.

"Nope." I let my gaze trail slowly down her body before returning to her face. "I was thinking more along the lines of…creative application."

She bit her bottom lip. "That sounds messy."

"Very messy," I agreed, my voice dropping lower. "Good thing hotel rooms come with showers."

A small sound escaped her throat. Not quite a laugh, not quite a moan. "You're so bad."

"You have no idea, but you're about to find out." I winked at her then stepped toward the register to make my purchase.

I paid for the chocolate sauce while Morgan waited by the door, clutching her wrapped book to her chest. When I rejoined her, our eyes met and the air between us shifted. The playful flirtation from moments ago had ignited into something hotter and more urgent.

"Ready to head back to our hotel?" I asked.

Desire was written all over her face. "God, yes."

The walk through the Venetian felt endless. My hand remained locked with hers, and by the time we made it outside and hailed a cab, the tension between us was thick enough to cut with a knife.

The ride took less than ten minutes but felt like an eternity. I paid the driver, grabbed Morgan's hand, and practically pulled her through the lobby to the elevators. The moment the doors closed and we were alone, I had her pressed against the wall, my mouth claiming hers in a kiss that was all heat and hunger and weeks of pent-up longing. She moaned into my mouth, one of her hands fisting in my shirt.

The elevator dinged far too soon, and the doors opened on our floor. We stumbled down the hallway, stopping twice so I could kiss her again because I couldn't help myself. When we finally reached her door, her hands shook so badly she could barely get the key card to work.

I took it from her, swiped it through the reader, and pushed the door open. As we entered the room and the door shut behind us, I reached for her, but she surprised me by moving out of my reach with a flirty grin I was starting to recognize as a precursor to her rocking my world.

She set the chocolate sauce and her still wrapped book on the dresser. "I'm going to change," she said.

I was tempted to tell her not to bother. My dick was hard as stone and I wanted her naked and underneath me as soon as humanly possible. But there was a seductive gleam in her eyes that told me she had something special planned, so I didn't argue.

Whatever it was she grabbed from her suitcase, she was careful to keep it hidden from view, then disappeared into the bathroom. While she was gone, I stripped off my suit jacket and shoes, then started unbuttoning my shirt. A few minutes later the bathroom door opened, and the moment I glanced in that direction my brain seemed to short-circuit.

Morgan emerged, looking like a fucking goddess. A vision in red lingerie designed specifically to destroy my self-control. Her brown hair tumbled in waves around her shoulders, framing a face flushed with anticipation. But it was what she wore—or barely wore—that was nothing short of sinful and made my mouth go dry.

Thin red straps framed her full breasts and left her nipples exposed so they peeked through provocatively. Sheer mesh hugged her stomach and accentuated her curves. More straps crisscrossed over her hips, leading to the small scrap of fabric that barely covered her mound. She was pure temptation, and I couldn't tear my eyes away.

"*Fuck me*," I breathed, nearly tripping over my discarded shoes as I moved toward her.

She laughed, a sultry sound that was like a stroke to my cock as she sauntered to the bed. I followed, but my gaze snagged on the chocolate sauce on the dresser. I grabbed it, setting it on the nightstand before I quickly stripped off the rest of my clothes then joined her on the bed where she was reclining back on the pillows, watching me with a hooded gaze.

I moved over her, and our lips met in a heated clash, my hands roaming her lush figure as we tangled in a frenzy of touches and kisses, elevating the raw need that had been simmering between us for weeks. I trailed my mouth along the side of her neck, over her collarbone, and skimmed my lips across the swell of her breasts. Her exposed, peaked nipples begged for attention, and she let out an impatient little moan as I drew the straps over her chest down, baring her completely.

Sitting up, I straddled her thighs and grabbed the jar, twisting it open. The thick chocolate sauce was perfect for drizzling, and I let a ribbon of it fall across one pebbled nipple, then the other, watching the dark syrup drip down her full breasts.

She stared up at me, biting her lip, eyes shimmering with anticipation. Holding her gaze, I lowered my mouth to her breast, my tongue sweeping across her nipple to collect the chocolate. The rich, sweet flavor, combined with the salt of her skin, made me groan against her breast.

I loved the outfit, but my patience evaporated. I tore through the mesh over her stomach with a growl. She inhaled a startled breath, but didn't protest as I repositioned myself so that I was kneeling between her spread legs, then I poured more chocolate in a trail from her chest down to where that small bit of fabric still covered her sex. Then, I licked it off, following the same path down to her lower stomach.

"You're so fucking delicious," I growled, my voice rough with need. "I want to devour you."

Her fingers knotted in my hair, pulling me back up for a deep kiss while her free hand reached down and fisted my stiff, aching cock. "Hmm, you taste like chocolate," she murmured, sliding her palm along my shaft and giving it a few firm strokes. "But I can't wait anymore, Liam. I need you so badly."

Her urgency matched mine, sending a spear of pure desire straight through me. I slid a hand between her legs, discovering snaps in her lingerie and I didn't hesitate to tear them open, along with the ones at her hip that allowed me to strip the outfit completely off her body so she was as naked as me. I lined up the head of my cock and thrust into her slick heat, burying myself to the hilt. We both groaned in pleasure and relief, her walls clenching around my dick.

I stilled, fighting for control so I didn't spill my load before she had the chance to orgasm. She felt too damn good after so long, it threatened to push me instantly over the edge. The only thing I wanted more than to come inside of Morgan was to watch her fall apart for me first.

Rising to my knees, I gripped her hips and pulled her lower half onto my lap, and she immediately wrapped her legs around my waist. Her body lay splayed before me, hair tousled, her skin smeared with chocolate, and as I began fucking her in earnest, her breasts bounced with each deep, hard thrust.

She clutched the bed covers, arousing sounds spilling from her lips with every roll of my hips elevating my own desire for her.

I groaned, moving faster, rougher. "You have no idea how much I needed this. How many times I've fantasized about spreading you out on my desk and sinking myself so deep inside you that all you feel is me. Those tight skirts you wear drive me insane, you know that?"

Lost in sensation, she moaned in response, but I needed to hear her say it.

I forced myself to stop and reached up to pinch her nipples, just hard enough to make her gasp and get her attention. "Answer me, Morgan. Do you know how crazy you make me in your form fitting suits and dresses?" I rolled her nipples between my fingers again, watching her squirm and feeling her pussy spasm around my dick, still buried deep inside her. "Do you know how badly my cock aches as I sit behind my desk, trying to act professional when you make me feel like a fucking animal?"

"Yes, I know," she cried out. "God, please keep fucking me."

I grinned and leaned over her, bracing my hands by her shoulders so that my face was only inches from hers. "And you like it, don't you? You like knowing the effect you have on me."

"Yes!" She reached around to my ass, gripping it hard enough that I could feel the bite of her nails. "Yes, I love knowing that you want me so much. I want you to bend me over your desk and fuck me because I think about it, too. I think about sinking to my knees under your desk every time I walk in there and how much I loved sucking you off and watching you lose control."

Holy shit. Her filthy confession unleashed something primal inside me, and I started to move again—harder this time, pounding into her with an intensity that bordered on savage. The headboard slammed against the wall in rhythm to my thrusts, but I couldn't stop. I needed this. I needed her.

She craved my unrestrained passion just as much, her voice taking on a desperate edge as she encouraged me to give her *more, more, more*!

My stomach muscles tightened as my climax approached, barreling through me like a freight train, and a hoarse groan rumbled up from my chest as I released inside her. Morgan was right there with me. Her legs tightened around my waist, her whole body shaking uncontrollably as she unraveled so beautifully beneath me with a soft cry of pleasure.

We clung to each other through the aftershocks, bodies slick and spent. I couldn't remember ever feeling more complete, or more content with another person.

Eventually, I forced myself to move and pulled out of her. I cleaned us both with a warm washcloth, pressing gentle kisses to her skin as I wiped away the remnants of chocolate and sex. She watched me through heavy-lidded eyes, a soft, sated smile playing at her lips.

After turning off the lights, I slid into bed beside her and pulled her into my arms. I closed my eyes, and as she let out a long sigh and relaxed against my chest, the truth hit me like the sharp clarity of an unexpected lightning strike, jolting through every part of me.

I loved this woman.

My eyes flew back open at that thought, staring into the darkness of the room as I waited for the panic to surface. The suffocating fear. The overwhelming urge to run that had defined my response to emotional intimacy for years now.

But nothing like that happened. There was no dread. No warning bells. I wasn't freaking out. This wasn't like our first night together where flight instinct had ruled my actions.

I felt…peaceful and happy.

I ran a hand down Morgan's bare back, her skin warm and soft beneath my palm, and pressed a kiss to the top of her head. For years, I'd convinced myself that Ivy was the one who got away. That if I'd just made better choices, worked fewer hours, said the right things, we could have had the future I'd envisioned. But lying here with Morgan in my arms, I knew with absolute certainty that I'd been wrong.

Ivy was never mine in the way Morgan was. If I'd ever felt a fraction of this connection with Ivy, I wouldn't have buried myself in my job. I wouldn't have chosen meetings and late nights at the office and endless deals over her. And she wouldn't have been open to the idea of falling in love with someone else if we'd had a strong relationship to begin with. Something worth fighting for, which in hindsight, neither of us had tried to do.

With Morgan, everything was different. The

thought of a future without her was unbearable, while the thought of a future with her filled me with a certainty I'd never experienced before. I wasn't afraid of this love because I knew, bone-deep, that I wouldn't repeat the same mistakes. I wouldn't let work consume me. Wouldn't let distance grow between us. And I would never take her for granted.

I wanted to build a life with her. Wanted to wake up beside her every morning. Learn all her quirks and habits and favorite things. I wanted to be the man she deserved.

And I intended to make that happen. We still had a few more days left at CES, but when we returned to New York things between us needed to change. Hopefully, Simon would have some answers from the forensic accountant and then, I wanted our relationship out in the open. I wanted to take her to dinner in our own city, introduce her to my friends, and sit beside her at family gatherings without worrying who might see. I wanted her woven into every part of my life.

And when I told her I loved her, it wasn't going to be in bed after sex. I wanted to do it right, in a way that made her feel special and treasured. She deserved our first "I love you" to be a moment she remembered for the rest of her life, and I intended to give her that when the time and place was right.

Morgan shifted in her sleep, burrowing closer, and I tightened my arms around her. My eyes drifted closed, and for the first time in years, falling asleep felt easy. Because I was exactly where I was supposed to be…with the woman I loved curled against my side, and a future full of possibilities stretching out before us.

CHAPTER TWENTY-TWO

Morgan

THE REST OF the week in Vegas flew by. While Liam and I spent our days at CES, our evenings belonged entirely to us. He insisted on taking me to the most upscale establishments, including dinner overlooking the Strip at the Eiffel Tower, and surprised me with tickets to a Cirque du Soleil show.

We rode the second-largest Ferris wheel in the world, wandered through an aquarium filled with sharks, and stood hand in hand watching the Bellagio Fountains. We even strolled through the Neon Museum, weaving between old iconic signs that still glowed with the magic of the city's past.

Every outing with Liam seemed like something straight out of movie. Romantic. Magical. And at night, when we slipped into my room and closed the door behind us, the connection between us only deepened and intensified. Whatever we were building between us, it wasn't just chemistry. It was something real, and I couldn't deny that something expanded inside me every time he touched me or looked at me like I was the only woman in the room for him.

There was a lightness to Liam the rest of the week. A softness around the edges I hadn't seen before. He seemed more open, as if being with me stripped away the weight and pieces of the past he'd been carrying for years. And I felt it, too, the growing sense that this wasn't just a whirlwind vacation fling.

I was falling for him, harder and deeper every day.

One night, after dinner in Vegas and a lazy evening of letting Liam worship my body, we ended up talking about what came next. Not in a rushed way, not with pressure, just honest clarity between us. We agreed that once we returned to New York, we wouldn't hide our relationship much longer. I knew things with my brother and father had to be handled carefully, but within the first week or two, when the time was right and things settled back into a normal routine after CES, we planned to have that conversation with them. To make our relationship official. To date openly. To live our lives without pretending we were just coworkers.

And as we packed our things on the final morning, preparing to fly home, a steady calm settled over me. I wasn't nervous. I wasn't uncertain. I knew exactly where we stood. By the time we left Vegas, I was secure in what we had. Secure in him. Whatever delicate steps we had to take at work until we were ready to reveal our relationship, whatever conversations lay ahead, none of it shook my confidence in us one bit.

Liam and I were on steady, unquestionable ground. And for the first time in a long time, I knew the future I wanted. And it was with him.

Everything went better than expected at the electronics show. There was obvious enthusiasm for our portable EV charger from representatives of companies that were interested in selling it for us when we launched the product. There was no doubt that this device was going to be a game changer for our company.

Back in New York on Monday morning, I looked forward to seeing Liam again in the office. Being with him in Vegas had felt so natural, so easy, that the idea of slipping back into pretending we were just coworkers made my heart sink a little. But I understood why we needed to be careful making thoughtful decisions about our relationship, instead of impulsive ones. There was Liam's investment in the company to consider, and neither one of us wanted to risk our professional reputations until we were ready to announce things on our terms.

As usual, I was one of the first people to arrive. Even Liam's office was dark. I settled at my desk, arranging my calendar for the day and getting caught up on important emails. I heard the elevator open multiple times over the next hour, followed by the murmured conversations of employees in the hallway.

My dad walked by at one point, talking to his assistant. He sent me a smile, already knowing the Vegas trip had been a success. Liam and I had a meeting scheduled with him and Parker to go over CES more in detail, but I'd kept him well updated while we were out of town.

Once the urgent emails were handled, I headed to the breakroom, desperate for caffeine. Someone had already brewed a pot and I grabbed a mug and filled it with coffee, then stirred in two sugars.

I heard someone enter, but before I could turn around strong arms slipped around my waist, pulling me back against a solid chest. Liam's lips brushed my neck, and I melted against him instinctively.

That reaction only lasted a second, though. I stiffened as I remembered where we were. I turned around and tried to step back, but I bumped into the counter and Liam caged me in with his arms on either side of me, a wolfish smile on his lips. Despite the risk of being caught, my heart rate accelerated and desire thrummed through me.

"We shouldn't do this here," I said, my eyes shifting over his shoulder to the open door. There was no one else around for now, but someone could walk in at any moment, and I didn't want them to find us in what could appear to be a compromising position.

"You're right." Liam released a low, regretful sigh as he stepped back, giving me space even though he clearly didn't want to. "I can't seem to help myself around you."

I laughed softly. "It's not easy for me, either."

"Good." He pushed his hands into his pockets, as if that would keep him from reaching out and touching me again. "So, I wanted to ask if you'd like to go with me to my sister-in-law's art show. It's the last Saturday of this month."

My eyes widened in surprise. "Your sister-in-law is an artist?"

He nodded, the corner of his mouth lifting in one of those irresistibly charming smiles of his. "She is. Fallon is insanely talented, and the gallery is donating half the proceeds to a women's shelter. My whole family will be there."

A flutter stirred in my chest. "Are you asking me as a friend or as your date?"

"As my date." His gaze softened, earnest and hopeful. "And as my official girlfriend. I know we'll be telling your family soon, probably by next week, so I want to make sure you keep that Saturday open. I'd like you to meet my family, too."

My heart gave a definite flip. "So…we're really doing this, huh?"

"Oh, we so are," he said with certainty.

"Then, yes," I said, smiling. "I would love to."

Liam's cell phone rang, pulling his attention from our conversation. He withdrew it from his pocket and glanced at the screen before giving me an apologetic look. "It's Simon. I'd better take it."

"Of course."

He walked out of the breakroom, picking up the call while I grabbed my cup of coffee and returned to my office. I found a list of potential vendors on my desk. I'd asked Jenny to compile the information from the people she met at CES, but I didn't expect her to get it to me so quickly.

Settling into my chair, I started to research each name on the list, but I didn't get very far before Liam appeared in my open doorway. I smiled automatically, but as he stepped inside, I immediately sensed a difference in him from just fifteen minutes ago in the breakroom, when he'd been happy and relaxed. Something in him had shifted. His shoulders were tight, his jaw tense, and there was a frown on his face.

Concerned, I stood and rounded my desk. "Hey. What's wrong?"

"Why do you think something's wrong?" he asked.

I folded my arms across my chest and raised a brow.

He grimaced and rubbed a hand along the back of his neck. "I guess you can already read me pretty well, huh?"

"Maybe." I gave him a teasing smile to lighten the mood. "Or maybe you're not as mysterious as you think."

He huffed a quiet laugh, but it didn't erase the tension in his body. "I'm fine," he said, almost dismissively. "Just some financial trouble with one of the companies we've invested in. Nothing to worry about."

His tone was casual, but his eyes shifted away from mine as he spoke. It was just for a moment, but it was enough to cause an uneasy knot to form in my stomach.

"Are you sure?" I asked.

"Yeah. I'll be fine."

His answer came too quickly, but I got the point and let it go. If it was related to another investment, it wasn't really any of my business anyway.

"How are you settling back into work at the office?" I asked, changing the subject instead. "Missing Vegas yet?"

His gaze dipped lower, where my blouse was unbuttoned just enough to show a hint of cleavage. "I miss *certain* things about Vegas."

Heat pooled in my belly and I grinned. "Well, I might be persuaded to give you some quality time with me here in New York as well. How about dinner tonight, at my place?"

Going to a restaurant would have been nice, but for now we needed to keep things low-key. And honestly, cooking dinner for him, then spending the night together, sounded like the perfect evening to me.

"Sure. I'll come by around six." He hesitated, eyes shifting away again. "But…the rest of my week might consist of some late nights. I've got some work to catch up on here and with Simon after being out of town last week."

There it was again. The tension, the distance, like something heavy was sitting on his shoulders.

"That's not a problem," I reassured him. "I'm still going to be here, even when work gets busy."

"I know, baby." He brushed a hand along my arm, before something tightened in his expression again.

"But I'm wondering, does anyone else besides Parker work late around here?"

The odd question caught me off guard. "Not usually. Everyone's out the door by six. Parker stays late sometimes, but that's about it."

"Just Parker, huh?" he asked again. "You sure about that?"

The intensity in Liam's eyes confused me, and I frowned. "Yes, I'm sure. Why?"

"Just curious." He stepped back, shutting down the conversation. "I have to go meet with Simon about that issue I mentioned. I'm not sure how long it's going to take, but I'll see you tonight."

"Okay," I said, hating the apprehension tightening my chest.

He left my office, and I sat back down at my desk. I attempted to concentrate on the vendor list but my mind lingered on Liam's strange behavior. He'd been distant, distracted, and clearly worried about something he didn't want to discuss.

No matter how hard I tried, I couldn't shake the sense that something bigger was going on. And until he decided to let me in, all I could do was wait, trust what we had, and try to keep my brain from spiraling into worst case scenarios.

CHAPTER TWENTY-THREE

Liam

THE WEIGHT OF the phone call I'd just had with Simon pressed down on my shoulders as I walked into his office. As I sat in the chair in front of his desk, the grim look on his face told me the in-person update wasn't going to be any better.

"I forwarded you the full report from the forensic accountant," he said, getting right to the point. "There's clear evidence of embezzlement."

My stomach in knots, I opened the email on my tablet while he sat quietly, giving me a moment as I flipped through each document with the swipe of my finger. The evidence was worse than I'd expected…page after page of inflated invoices, manipulated numbers, and money being funneled into accounts designed to hide the fact that it was being siphoned out fraudulently. It had been happening before we ever invested in the company, but the moment our money hit the books, the withdrawals had increased.

Worse, most of our initial investment was already gone.

Simon leaned forward. "Did you find out who works evenings? The timestamps of the transfers always occurred after office hours, which is the only clue we have right now about who is taking the money."

I exhaled sharply, guilt eating at me as I remembered the way I'd manipulated Morgan into giving me that information. "I think it's Parker," I said, hating to admit out loud that Morgan's stepbrother was most likely responsible. If true, this discovery was going to crush her.

"He's the only person Morgan mentioned that works late at the office," I went on. "And last month, he had a problem with my plan to increase the marketing budget because he was concerned about the manufacturing costs. That didn't make any sense at the time, but if he already knew the money wasn't there…"

"It makes sense now because he stole it." Simon's voice hardened, outrage simmering just beneath the surface.

I understood his anger, but I was more conflicted than him. My relationship with Morgan aside, I genuinely liked Parker. He was a good man, a smart man. I just didn't understand why he'd do something like this.

Simon stood and paced to the window, his shoulders rigid. "We need to catch him in the act."

I nodded in agreement, expecting him to suggest surveillance or more accounting reviews. Instead, he said, "I say we invest another million."

I stared at him in shock. "You want to give him *more* money to steal?"

Simon's jaw tightened. "I want to hire a computer programmer to set up a back door in GalvaTech's system so we have the ability to monitor the account in real time. If he makes a move to embezzle more, we'll have irrefutable proof. Timestamps, login credentials, everything."

Logically, I knew it was the right move but it still felt like a betrayal of not just Morgan, but her whole family. They'd welcomed me with kindness and appreciation for what I could bring to the company. Samuel had treated me with respect from the beginning. And I hated that I couldn't confide in Morgan, that I was keeping something so monumental from her that could potentially damage our fragile relationship. But for now, I knew I didn't have a choice.

I also couldn't allow Parker to keep draining the business and stealing the money we'd invested in the company. And stealing from his own family too.

"Okay," I said finally. "I'll talk to Samuel about investing another million tomorrow. You handle the programmer."

Simon nodded, satisfied. I wished I felt the same.

All I could do now was hope that when the truth came out, it didn't destroy a good family—and didn't completely shatter the woman I loved.

✧ ✧ ✧

ONCE THE BACK door system was in place and the extra money invested, it took three days. Three days of waiting, watching the system and financial accounts, and me, hoping—stupidly—that we were wrong. That it was someone else working late and moving the money around. That Parker wasn't cable of embezzling from his own family.

But late last night, a transfer went through, moved to one of the shell accounts we'd identified. Fifty grand. And the programmer traced it cleanly back to one computer. Parker's. Logged in under his name, with his passcode, with his IP address. There was no doubt any longer who was transferring the funds for their own personal gain.

Simon wanted to contact the authorities immediately, but I talked him into waiting a couple of days, to give me a chance to handle it a different way. I wasn't even sure what I planned to do, but I knew it had to start with telling Morgan so she wasn't blindsided.

My heart sat like a rock in my chest as I arrived at her apartment. She'd been out of the office most of the day in meetings, and I was grateful because I knew she'd pick up on the fact that something was bothering me right away.

This was our second dinner at her place this week. Last time, I'd been able to push my concerns about Parker aside and just be present with her. We'd had an enjoyable meal, we'd conversed and kept things light, ending the night with her bent over the back of the couch and me losing my mind inside her. I wanted that again. I wanted to grab her, bury my face in her neck, and pretend that I wasn't about to fracture her entire world.

But I couldn't. It was bad enough that I'd kept everything from her until now. The guilt I carried was festering inside me. I couldn't hold back the truth any longer.

I forced myself to knock, and she opened the door with a smile that made my chest ache. I caught the scent of garlic and tomato sauce, but as delicious as the meal smelled, I had zero appetite.

She greeted me with a kiss, but she must have sensed my reluctance because she pulled back, her smile instantly fading. Her hand came up to cup my cheek, her thumb brushing my skin.

"Liam?" Her gaze searched mine. "What's wrong?"

It was terrifying how in sync we were. How well she already knew me. But what I had to tell her tonight was going to be the first true test of our relationship.

"We need to talk," I said, my voice rougher than I'd intended.

"Okay…" She looked confused, and concerned. "Do you want a drink first? Or dinner?"

I shook my head. "No, not yet."

I took her hand. It felt small and warm in mine, and I gave it a gentle squeeze before leading her over to the brown suede couch in the living room. I sat down and pulled her onto the cushion next to me, turning so I could face her fully.

Her posture was visibly tense. "Liam, you're scaring me. What's going on?"

I kept hold of her hand, rubbing my thumb across her knuckles, trying to find the words. Every way I'd rehearsed this in my head sounded wrong. Everything about this was fucking gut-wrenching and I had to force myself to speak.

"There's something I need to tell you," I said, swallowing hard. "Something I should have told you sooner but I was waiting until I had proof."

Her brow furrowed. "Proof of what?"

"GalvaTech has been losing money for the past year, well before Simon and I invested. It's been well hidden up until now, but our forensic accountant found it."

Shock transformed her features. "Forensic accountant? What are you talking about? I didn't know you—"

"We kept it from you," I admitted, hating how the words hung heavy between us. "Simon and I, we noticed some discrepancies in the financial reports, and we decided to investigate it ourselves without telling you or your family."

Hurt flared in her eyes, sharp and immediate. *Fuck.* We'd barely scratched the surface of what I had to tell her, and she was already in pain.

"The losses have gotten worse since our investment," I pressed on. "And that extra million Simon and I just put into the company has already started to disappear."

"No." She abruptly stood, shaking her head in denial like she could physically reject the information. "That can't be right. I don't believe anyone at GalvaTech would do such a thing."

"It's not just anyone," I said, also getting to my feet. "It's Parker."

She froze, staring at me in stark disbelief. She didn't even have to say a word for me to know that she thought I was insane for suggesting such a thing.

"It's true." I reached for her hand, but she stepped back, the rejection hitting me like a punch to the gut. "I wouldn't accuse him without being certain, Morgan. You know me better than that."

"It's not possible," she said in a calm voice that did nothing to soften the anger in her eyes. "Parker wouldn't do that. This is our family's company. He wouldn't hurt us that way. And he makes good money. If he ever needed help, he'd come to us. Or me. This doesn't make sense. You're clearly mistaken."

"The programmer we hired set up a trace on the new funds," I explained, keeping my tone even despite the frustration building in my chest. "It led straight back to Parker. His computer. His login credentials. There's no doubt."

Her eyes narrowed. "A forensic accountant *and* a computer programmer were hired and given access to our computer systems without our permission?" she asked incredulously.

I knew she was deflecting, unable to wrap her mind around the bombshell I'd just dropped. I hated that she was looking at me as if I was the enemy.

"The contract that I signed with your father makes me a partner in the business, Morgan," I said. "I'm authorized to access everything at GalvaTech."

"That doesn't make it right!" Her voice rose, sharp with betrayal, her hands clenching at her sides. "You should have told us what your suspicions were."

I exhaled a deep, steadying breath when I felt anything but. "We didn't know who was doing the embezzling. Keeping it quiet seemed like the best way to find out who was responsible without tipping anyone off."

Her jaw dropped, her eyes widening with fresh hurt. "Are…are you saying you suspected *me*?"

"No," I said, stepping closer and placing my hands on her shoulders before she could move away. "No, baby. I *never* thought it was you. But you have to understand why we kept it quiet. It's Parker. Would you have told me that he often works late if I'd been honest about the money transfers occurring in the evenings?"

She jerked out of my grip, renewed anger flashing across her features. "You tricked me into telling you that! I never would have pointed the finger at Parker if I'd known why you were asking."

"That's the point," I said. "We had to keep it quiet because you're family. I knew you'd protect the thief if it turned out to be one of your family members."

"Don't call him a thief!" she snapped. "Parker isn't like that."

"He's stolen hundreds of thousands of dollars!" I

said just as heatedly.

We were both upset and shouting, and I could feel the situation spiraling out of control. I hated every single second of this conversation. Morgan turned away, walking the length of the living room as if she needed to put distance between us. Each step away from me felt like a mile.

"How long?" she asked, her voice suddenly emotionless.

I would have preferred the anger, but this sudden cold, stoic distance felt like the door was closing on our relationship.

"What?" I asked, the despair washing over me, making my brain lag.

She crossed her arms over her chest and lifted her chin. "How long have you been investigating this?"

I knew in that moment that I was about to deliver a devastating blow to our relationship, but I couldn't bring myself to lie to her. There were already too many lies of omission weighing on me, hovering between us.

"Since before Vegas," I admitted quietly.

The devastated look on her face was more potent and raw this time, and I cursed under my breath, hating that I was responsible for putting it there.

"You knew the whole time we in Vegas together?" she whispered, her voice trembling as memories flashed in her eyes—the intimacy we'd shared, the connection we'd built. "All those moments…the dates, the nights…you were keeping this from me?"

"I knew something was wrong with the accounting," I said, pushing my fingers through my hair. "But I didn't know it was Parker until now. I swear, I wanted to tell you. I hated holding back. But I needed proof first, to protect everyone, including you."

"But you didn't tell me," she said in a flat tone. "This company is my life, Liam. And you didn't trust me enough to let me in. Now you expect me to just take your word that Parker is embezzling money? Why should I?"

I understood her point. I'd known keeping this from her was a betrayal, but I'd done it anyway, prioritizing the investigation over us. I stood there feeling helpless, searching for words to make this right, but none came. There was no defense that would soften this blow for her.

She walked over to the apartment door and opened it. "I want you to go."

I didn't miss the glisten of tears in her eyes, and panic rose in my chest. "Morgan, I can't leave like this." The thought of walking out terrified me because I knew this could end us. I couldn't lose her. Not now, not after realizing how much she meant to me.

I thought about telling her that I loved her, but that felt too much like emotional manipulation right now. It wasn't the time or the place, and this situation was not how I wanted her to hear those words for the first time. And my biggest fear was that she'd reject them, anyway.

"I don't have anything else to say to you right now," she said, her voice breaking on the words, her sadness palpable. "I just need…space. I need you to *go.*"

The emotional plea in her eyes broke me. I couldn't push her, not when she looked so fragile, so vulnerable. Slowly, I walked toward her, my steps as heavy as my heart. Stopping beside her, I cupped her cheek gently, brushing away a stray tear with my thumb when she didn't pull away.

"I'll go for now," I told her, holding her gaze. "But this isn't over, sweetheart. Not the conversation and definitely not us."

I forced myself to walk out. I had to believe we could fix this. Work through the hurt, the secrets I'd kept…it was the only thing that kept me moving as I heard the door shut behind me, solid and final.

CHAPTER TWENTY-FOUR

Morgan

I WAS PROBABLY lucky to have made it through twenty-six years of life without ever experiencing a betrayal like the one tearing me apart now, but that didn't make the rest of the night any easier. I tossed and turned, my dreams a messy, confusing mix of wanting Liam, yelling at him, and watching him walk away from me for good, leaving me alone with nothing but the echo of his accusations.

By morning, I was a grumpy disaster, nursing a too-strong cup of coffee in a kitchen that still smelled faintly of the garlic bread I'd made for our dinner. I'd planned on a simple night with Liam. A nice meal, maybe a movie, definitely ending the evening tangled up together in my bed.

So much for my best-laid plans. Instead, Liam had dropped a bomb that had left me gutted, furious, and impossibly confused. And in the warm morning light, nothing felt less painful. If anything, the hurt burrowed deeper.

I was devastated that he kept the money discrepancies from me while we were in Vegas. That trip meant something to me. It felt like we'd grown closer in a real way. I'd opened myself up to him, trusted him, and believed he'd trusted me in return. Now, I couldn't help but look back on those days through the lens of deceit. The whole time, he'd been keeping something huge from me.

Then there was Parker. No matter what Liam said, I couldn't wrap my head around the idea of my stepbrother stealing from us. Parker could do it, sure. He was brilliant with computers and anything tech related. If anyone could get away with embezzling, it was him. But why would he do such a thing? Unless…unless there was some reason I didn't know about. Something that had made him desperate enough to—

No. I couldn't think like that.

Frustrated with my spiraling thoughts, I finished my coffee and dressed for work. Thanks to not sleeping, I arrived even earlier than usual. The office was quiet, lights dimmed, the hallways hushed.

I headed toward my office like I would any other morning. But when I reached the door, I stopped. My gaze drifted further down the hall to Parker's office.

I knew he kept it locked. But I also knew my father had spare keys in his desk to every office, just in case anyone got locked out.

Don't do this.

I told myself to just go into my own office and stick to my conviction that Parker was innocent. I could talk to Dad about Liam's accusations today, and he'd know how to handle the situation. There was no need to snoop through my stepbrother's things like some kind of paranoid detective.

But I still lingered in the hallway, biting my lip, staring at that closed door, while more intrusive thoughts found their way into my conscience. How Becca's credit card had been denied the night of my birthday. How Parker told her to scale back on Christmas gifts for Gracie and he'd had Becca cancel their babymoon. How he'd reacted that night when we'd been at my parents for dinner and Becca had mentioned them buying a bigger house to accommodate their growing family.

No matter how much I tried to talk myself out of it, I couldn't pass up the opportunity to look. Truthfully, the doubt that Liam had planted was already taking root, whispering at the back of my mind in tortuous ways, and I knew I'd spend the entire day wondering. I knew I could ask Liam to view the reports from the forensic accountant, but I wanted to do this on my own. Cold, hard numbers wouldn't make as much sense to me as looking around Parker's office for a reason why.

I told myself no one had to know. I could take a quick look around, confirm that there was nothing incriminating to find, and leave, my conscience clear.

Five minutes later, spare key in hand, I let myself into Parker's office.

Everything was neat and organized, as always. His

shelves were lined with Lego sets he'd built, little shrines to his nerdy hobbies. Two monitors sat on his desk beside neat stacks of papers. A filing cabinet stood behind it, topped with framed photos of Becca and Gracie.

Exhaling a deep breath, I moved to the filing cabinet first. I flicked through the folders, hating that I was betraying Parker's trust just by being in here, going through his things. By letting Liam's accusation create enough doubt to make me search for evidence I desperately hoped didn't exist.

Still, I searched. The filing cabinet contained nothing suspicious, just details of past and current projects, technical specifications, and vendor contracts. The stack of papers on his desk were all related to the EV charger. Everything was exactly what it should be. I wanted to leave, to forget that I ever came in here, but I knew it would drive me crazy if I left before checking everywhere.

Pulling open the top drawer of his desk, I expected to see nothing more than pens, paperclips, and Post-it notes. Those things were there, but it was the small plastic baggie of white powder that made me freeze as I stared in wide-eyed horror.

My brain rejected it immediately. *No. It can't be what it looks like.*

There was no way that Parker had drugs in his office. No. Way.

But my excuses had finally reached their limit. I'd never touched recreational drugs in my life, but I was certain that's exactly what I was looking at. My breath went shallow. My hands shook as I picked up the baggie, my denial crumbling with every heartbeat. I shut the drawer hard and shoved the bag into the pocket of my blazer. I didn't look through the other drawers, suddenly afraid of what else I might find.

I rushed out of Parker's office, pausing only long enough to lock the door behind me so no one else could wander inside and discover whatever other secrets might be hiding in there. I grabbed my purse, my mind reeling as I ran to the elevator, glad that no one else was around to see me because I was sure my panic and confusion were stamped all over my face.

Why would Parker have drugs? And what kind of drug was this, anyway?

I was halfway to his house before it even occurred to me that I probably had an illegal substance in my pocket and what that could mean if I got pulled over. That had never happened to me. I'd never gotten so much as a speeding ticket, but suddenly I couldn't stop imagining a police officer asking me to step out of the car, finding the baggie, and slapping handcuffs on my wrists.

I drove like someone's grandmother, going exactly the speed limit, coming to complete stops at every sign, my hands gripping the wheel at ten and two. Meanwhile, my heart raced so fast I felt light-headed.

By the time I pulled into Parker's driveway, I was a complete mess.

It was barely seven in the morning. I knew he'd be

getting ready to leave for work soon, probably eating breakfast with Becca and Gracie before heading out. Under normal circumstances, I never would have shown up unannounced this early. But I couldn't wait. I was too freaked out, too desperate for answers and explanations. I needed to know the truth, *right now*.

At the door, I didn't bother with the doorbell. I pounded my fist against the wood, each hit fueled by the nervous energy coursing through me. It took a couple of minutes, but Becca opened the door. She was in pajama pants and an oversized t-shirt that stretched over her pregnant belly, hair tousled, blinking at me in sleepy confusion.

"Morgan?" She frowned at me. "What are you doing here so early?"

"I need to talk to Parker." I stepped past her into the house without waiting to be invited in.

She closed the door and followed me into the living room, looking more awake now, worry creasing her forehead. "Is something wrong?"

"I just…I need to talk to him," I repeated, glancing around impatiently. "It's important."

"He's in the shower," Becca said, her concern increasing based on my own erratic behavior. "What's going on, Morgan? Are you okay?"

No, I was far from okay. I'd found drugs in my stepbrother's office. And there was a possibility—an awful, terrifying, *real* possibility—that Liam wasn't wrong about the money.

But I couldn't put this on Becca. Not when she

was pregnant. Not until I knew the truth about everything.

I exhaled a deep breath and forced myself to calm down. "I'm okay," I lied. "I just need to talk to Parker about something personal. Please, tell him I'm here."

"Okay," she said, and disappeared down the hall.

I sat down on the couch while I waited, but I couldn't relax. My foot tapped restlessly, and I picked at my nails. The baggie in my pocket felt like a lead weight, despite it being so light.

A short while later Parker walked in without Becca, which I was grateful for. This wasn't a confrontation I wanted to have with him in front of her. His hair was damp and he was wearing a suit. There was obvious concern on his face because I'd never shown up at their house this early, but other than that he looked completely normal. There was no sign that anything was off with him, just a slight stiffness in his movements, like when his back pain flared up.

I stood as he approached, searching his eyes for any hint that he was high, but they were clear.

"What's wrong?" he asked, brows furrowed as he stared at me. "Are you okay?"

His worry hit me hard. Classic Parker, always putting others first. We'd been so close for so long, how had I missed this? My heart ached as I pulled the baggie from my pocket for him to see.

"No, Parker. I'm not okay," I said, my voice trembling with a mix of hurt and anger. "Are you?"

He blinked, his expression going blank for a split

second. When his eyes met mine again, they were guarded, and I could feel my heart cracking in my chest.

"What is that?" he asked, no inflection in his tone.

Anger surged through me. How could he pretend not to know? "Seriously?" I asked in a sharp tone, realizing I was going to have to be brutal with him. "That's how you're going to play this? Are you going to deny the embezzling too? Liam told me everything. About the missing money, and how it all leads back to you."

Parker paled. His mouth opened, but no sound came out.

"Parker, talk to me," I pleaded, doing my best to shove down the anger, my voice softening with desperation. "What the hell is going on? This isn't you. I know it's not. Just…explain, *please*."

For moment, he said nothing, but then, his face crumpled.

My strong, confident stepbrother fell apart in front of my eyes, his shoulders shaking as he buried his face in his hands, the muffled sounds of his crying filling the room. I stared in shock as he sank down onto the couch, but the sound of a particularly harsh sob spilled from him, and I moved to his side as my chest squeezed tight. I placed a hand on his back as he told me everything without looking at me.

"I'm sorry," he gasped, trying to wipe away his tears, but they fell too fast. "I'm so fucking sorry, Morgan. Oh God, it wasn't supposed to come to this.

I…I didn't think I'd ever be an addict, but when I hurt my back a couple of years ago and had to have surgery, I was given Oxy. It was the only thing that helped, but only if I took it all the time. You know it took months for me to recover, and I took the pills constantly. I *needed* them to function."

I thought back to that time in our lives. I was worried about him when he had the surgery and could barely walk or move without wincing in pain. It took a long time for him to recover, and ever since, he still had occasional pain in the area.

"I swear, I didn't even realize I was addicted to the meds. I took them for the pain. I *had* to. But then, as the pain got better, the doctor stopped writing my prescriptions. He told me to wean myself off, as if it was *so* easy. And I tried, Morgan. I swear, I *tried.*"

He lifted his gaze to mine, and the shame in his eyes made me want to cry with him. "I thought I was strong enough, you know? I didn't have the pain anymore, so it was just my mind working against me. I thought my willpower would be enough, but it just wasn't. All I could think about were the pills. I couldn't feel happy without them. I couldn't *function* without them."

"What happened next?" I asked, wondering how he went from prescription narcotics to whatever was in the baggie.

"I started buying pills when I could, but Oxy is hard to get, and I couldn't consistently get it. So, I had to turn to something else."

His eyes shifted to the baggie still in my hand, and there was a longing beneath the shame that truly horrified me. He was no longer crying, but he looked destroyed by his own story.

"What is this, Parker?"

He swallowed hard. "It's…it's heroin."

I dropped it on the coffee table, unable to stand touching the thing.

"I've been using it for over a year now, sinking more and more money into it. I've neglected other things, and it's all just snowballed. Now, I have massive debt. Credit cards, loans, the mortgage. We were about to lose the house the first time I took money from GalvaTech, and I was desperate. Then, there are the men I get the drugs from. These are bad people, Morgan, dangerous people. They threatened Becca and Gracie."

My blood ran cold, fear gripping me as I imagined the danger to them.

"So, you understand, right? I had to take the money. I hated myself for it, but I had to protect Becca and Gracie. I couldn't let them pay for my mistakes, my weakness."

I nodded slowly, squeezing his hand. I understood, as much as someone who'd never gone through addiction could. He was drowning in it, buried under debt and fear, making panicked choices while facing the consequences of his bad decisions. But how had I missed this? We saw each other almost daily. Our family was tight. How did this slip by me?

"Why didn't you tell me?" I asked, my voice cracking with hurt as I gripped his hand tighter. "I would have helped, Parker. We all would have. You didn't have to go through this alone."

His eyes were red and tormented, making me flinch at the depth of his pain. "I couldn't," he whispered raggedly. "I couldn't admit it to anyone. Not even myself at first. The shame and guilt, it was too much. I'm supposed to be the strong one, you know? And Becca…she has no idea. She doesn't know I've ruined everything. Our life, our future."

"It's not your fault," I said firmly, pulling him into a hug, holding him tight as he clung back. "Addiction is a disease, Parker, not a weakness. It messes with your brain, no matter how smart or strong you are. You need help, *real* help, and I'm going to make sure you get it. Rehab, therapy, whatever it takes. You're not alone. We'll figure this out together, and you're going to be okay."

A broken sound ripped from him as he tightened his arms around me, squeezing so hard it was tough to breathe, but I didn't pull away. I'd do anything for him.

"I love you, Parker," I said, keeping my voice steady and strong, even as my world felt like it was crumbling right alongside his. "We're family. We'll get through this."

It was a promise I intended to keep.

CHAPTER TWENTY-FIVE

Liam

I HADN'T BEEN spending much time at my office at the investment firm lately, but that's where I headed this morning. Part of me wanted to go straight to GalvaTech, to see Morgan, to try and fix what I'd broken last night. But a bigger part of me worried she wouldn't want to see me at all.

I had no idea where we stood after our conversation. And I was pretty sure it couldn't have gone worse.

My own bruised feelings had mostly faded overnight, replaced by a different kind of ache. The kind that came from knowing the woman I loved was in pain, and I was part of the reason why.

She'd lashed out at me, defensive and angry. Maybe I shouldn't have kept the investigation from her, but I knew the real problem wasn't my secrecy. It was Parker. If I'd accused anyone else of embezzlement, she would have been upset but ultimately understood my position.

But her stepbrother? That was different. That realization cut deep.

She might not have wanted to believe it, but Morgan knew me well enough to know I wouldn't lie about something like this. Which meant she was probably more torn up about it than she'd let on last night. And soon she'd know for certain I was telling the truth.

I had a meeting scheduled with Samuel that afternoon to tell him everything and show him the reports and proof. I was dreading that conversation almost as much as I'd dreaded telling Morgan.

This whole situation was a nightmare. I'd never gotten so personally invested in a company before. Some people might call that a mistake, but I couldn't bring myself to regret it. I cared about these people. About the company. About making this work.

That's why I hated being the one to bring Parker's crimes to light. But what choice did I have? Let him keep stealing? Watch GalvaTech slowly bleed out from the inside?

What I needed to figure out before the meeting was what came next. The contract Simon and I signed could be broken under certain specific conditions. Embezzlement definitely qualified. We could pull our investment and walk away without any repercussions.

I knew that's what Simon wanted. He'd said as much in our brief conversation this morning. But he was leaving the final decision to me since I was the one who'd been working closely with GalvaTech these past months.

Breaking the contract was the smart business move. We'd already invested significant money and now, even more would be needed to achieve our goals if I kept working with the company. But if we pulled out now, GalvaTech would go bankrupt. Most of the money had already been spent or embezzled, so Samuel would probably have to sell the company to return our investment.

A ruthless businessman wouldn't hesitate. But that wasn't me. I started this angel investment firm with Simon because I wanted to help other businesses succeed. Even without the emotional attachment I felt toward the whole Starling family, I wouldn't be quick to walk away and leave a company in ruins over the actions of one employee.

Factor in the way the collapse of the company would devastate Morgan, and I knew I wouldn't be able to do it.

I was sitting at my desk, staring into space as I contemplated my options with GalvaTech when my office door opened. I glanced up, expecting to see Simon or my assistant, but my heart skipped a beat when I met Morgan's captivating green eyes. They were misty, like she was fighting tears. Her face was pale, her expression distraught.

I was out of my chair and rounding my desk before she made it more than a few steps into the office. "Morgan." Her name came out rough. "What are you doing here?"

As I moved closer, she seemed to collapse inward,

shoulders sagging, knees going weak. I caught her, pulling her against my chest without hesitation. She buried her face in my shirt and took a deep, shuddering breath. There were no sobs, no dramatic crying. Just quiet tears that somehow felt more heartbreaking.

But the fact that she was here now gave me hope for us.

"I'm so sorry," I said, running my fingers through her soft hair. "I didn't mean to hurt you. I never should have kept the truth from you."

"No." She pulled back just enough to look up at me, and I gently brushed away the tears streaking her cheeks. "It's not just that. I wish you'd told me, yes, but I came here because…"

Her voice cracked and I pulled her to the client chairs in front of my desk, shifting them so that they were facing each other and urging her to sit. I took a seat in front of her, so close that our knees were touching. I didn't let go of her hands.

"Tell me," I said gently.

"It's Parker." She sniffled and gulped but didn't start crying again. "You were right about the embezzlement, but it's so much worse than just stealing from the company."

I couldn't imagine how it could get any worse than a man betraying his own family for money. But as she explained about the pills after his surgery, the addiction that spiraled into heroin use, the mounting debts and threats from dealers, I realized she was absolutely right. This was so much more complicated than simple greed. Now, knowing desperation and fear and addiction had driven his choices, it made sense in a tragic way.

"I just don't know how I missed the signs." Morgan's voice was small, defeated, and guilt was written all over her face. "How could I not see that he was struggling?"

I squeezed her hands. "He's obviously high-functioning, even on the drugs. I've spent plenty of time around him over the past couple months, and I never saw any classic signs that he was using. You said even Becca doesn't know, right?" I asked, and Morgan nodded miserably. "If his own wife doesn't know, you can't blame yourself for missing it."

"I can't help it." Her chin quivered. "I hate knowing he's been struggling and drowning in debt for years because of his addiction and I had no idea. I would've helped him, Liam. If he'd just told me—"

"You're going to help him now," I said firmly. "It's not too late. We'll figure this out together."

"I'm sorry," she whispered, fresh tears spilling down her cheeks as she looked away in embarrassment. "About yesterday. I know I overreacted, said things I didn't mean—"

"Stop." I cupped her face in my hands, making her look at me. "Forget about yesterday. You were protecting your family. I get it. And maybe I should have handled things differently from the start. I should have trusted you with the truth instead of keeping you in the dark."

"No, I understand why you didn't tell me." She took a shaky breath. "I hate to admit it, but it might have been for the best. I never would have suspected Parker. If you'd told me about the missing money early on, I might have mentioned it to him without thinking. I could have tipped him off, given him time to cover his tracks better, and he needed to be caught and held accountable. You were right. I was just too angry and hurt to see that last night." She pulled one hand free to wipe at her eyes. "God, what a mess."

"We'll figure it out," I promised her, knowing I'd be by her side the entire time. "What does Parker want to do? Has he agreed to get help?"

She nodded. "He wants to go to rehab. I'm going to help him find a good facility, somewhere that specializes in opioid addiction." She let out a bitter laugh. "The irony is, getting caught might have saved his life. He also said the dealers were getting more aggressive with their threats. He was terrified but saw no way out."

"And the embezzlement?"

"He wants to confess everything to my dad. Face whatever consequences that come." Morgan's voice steadied slightly. "I told him I'd be there with him when he does it. He shouldn't have to go through that alone."

Pride swelled in my chest. Even after everything—the lies, the betrayal, the heartbreak—Morgan's first instinct was to support her family.

"When are you telling Samuel?" I asked.

"This afternoon. I wanted to talk to you first." She met my eyes, vulnerable and open in a way that made my throat tight. "I needed to apologize. And I needed you to know that I trust you. Even when it's hard, even when the truth hurts, I trust you."

The weight that had been pressing in on my chest since last night finally lifted. "I love you," I said, the words spilling out before I could stop them.

Her eyes widened in surprise. "What?"

Shit. This probably wasn't the best timing, but I couldn't take it back now. And honestly, I didn't want to hold on to these feelings any longer.

"I love you, Morgan Starling," I repeated, stronger this time. "I know you're dealing with a crisis and we just had our first real fight, but I need you to know that I love you. And I'm not going anywhere. Whatever happens with Parker and GalvaTech and all of this, we'll face it together."

For a moment she just stared at me, lips parted in shock. Then she launched herself forward, wrapping her arms around my neck and kissing me hard.

"I love you, too," she whispered against my lips. "I love you so much."

I pulled her closer, deepening the kiss, pouring everything I felt into it. Relief and love and gratitude that she was there, that we were okay, that we'd survived our first real test.

When we finally broke apart, both breathing hard, Morgan rested her forehead against mine. "We're going to get through this," she said. Not a question, but a statement of fact.

"Yeah," I agreed, smiling at her. "We are."

Because now I knew for certain, whatever challenges came our way, we'd face them together. And that made all the difference.

CHAPTER TWENTY-SIX

Morgan

TWO WEEKS HAD passed since I learned about Parker's troubles, and the fallout had been rough for everyone.

He'd come clean to Becca the same day that I visited the house, and she was devastated. She felt the same guilt that I did for not noticing, but there was a lot of anger inside of her as well. I couldn't blame her for that. His actions had put her and Gracie in danger, *and* he'd screwed up their finances so badly that they were on the brink of ruin. There were so many lies between them, and it had left their marriage in a rocky state.

But Becca was strong, and she loved Parker. I was hopeful they'd work things out, especially since Parker had agreed to enter rehab. That willingness to get help, to actively change, had gone a long way toward mending the rift between them. It would take time, though. A lot of time.

On the other hand, my relationship with Liam had never been stronger. After we'd made up in his office and confessed our love for each other, we'd decided we were done hiding our relationship. No more sneaking around, no more pretending at work.

Given all the shock and drama surrounding Parker's situation, news of my relationship with Liam barely registered with my family. Which was a relief. My father, Faith, and everyone else were happy for us.

Tonight, I was going to meet the rest of Liam's family. We were going to Fallon's art show, and I was currently in the shower at Liam's apartment, getting ready for the evening. I'd been spending most of my time here lately, more than at my own place.

The sound of the bathroom door opening made me smile. A moment later, the shower door opened and my very naked, and very erect, boyfriend stepped in behind me. I turned to face him, taking in the wolfish grin on his face.

"Do you mind if I join you?" he asked.

I laughed. "You're already in here."

His eyes sparkled sinfully. "Well, I couldn't risk you saying no."

His hands slid around to grab my ass, pulling me flush against his body. His lips met mine and I moaned into his kiss, feeling the hard length of his cock pressing between us. My fingers tangled in his hair, already getting damp from the spray, and I nipped at his bottom lip.

He pressed me against the cool tile wall, then bent down to capture a nipple in his mouth.

"Liam," I gasped, my pussy clenching with need as

his teeth grazed the sensitive peak before he moved to my other breast.

His hand slipped between my legs, two fingers sliding easily inside me.

"So wet for me already," he murmured against my skin, his tongue swirling around my nipple. "You're always so eager and ready for my cock."

I shuddered at his dirty talk, heat flooding through me and making my thoughts hazy. But his fingers weren't enough. I needed more. I needed him.

"Liam," I begged, spreading my legs wider. "I want you inside me."

He straightened and lifted me off the ground without warning, and I let out a surprised squeak. My legs automatically wrapped around his hips as he positioned me against the wall, his cock pressing insistently at my entrance.

His tongue swept into my mouth as he lowered me onto his shaft, filling me in the way I yearned for. I whimpered, my legs tightening around him, my heels digging into his ass. In this position, I couldn't do much but hold on as he moved me up and down the tile wall, each deep thrust stealing my breath.

His movements were rough and fast, taking me hard, exactly the way I loved. My eyes closed, and I felt everything. The stretch of my pussy around him. The pleasure of being filled. The possessive grip of his hands. The delicious friction. It was so much. So overwhelming and perfect that I let my orgasm consume me.

With one final deep thrust, he came hard, too. We clung to each other as aftershocks rolled through us both. In moments like this, it was hard to believe we'd had such a rocky start. I tried not to dwell on it. The missteps of the past didn't matter anymore. There was only a bright future ahead of us now.

We finished our shower and got ready for the art show. We were cutting it close on time, but we managed to get out the door on schedule.

"So, how did the meeting with my father go?" I asked as Liam drove us to the gallery.

He'd spent the past few days with my father, hammering out the final details of a new contract necessary to keep GalvaTech going. I hadn't been involved in the negotiations—conflict of interest, given my relationship with Liam—but I was dying to know what they'd decided.

"We signed the new contract today," Liam said. "Your father drives a hard bargain. He got me to agree to invest another three million in the company."

His eyes flicked to me, and I smiled. I knew the truth behind that "hard bargain". Liam cared about the businesses he invested in. And I was a huge part of the reason he was pouring more money into GalvaTech instead of walking away like Simon had wanted. Liam knew what the company meant to me. What my family meant to me. So he wasn't abandoning us, despite what Parker had done.

"That brings our total investment to seven million," he continued. "The agreement is that when the

EV charger launches—and it will be successful—we'll be paid back over a five year period. Other than that, it's going to be an equal partnership."

I placed my hand on his thigh and squeezed. "You're my hero, you know that?"

He flashed me a teasing smile. "You're going to make me blush."

"I'm serious, Liam. You didn't have to do this. You could have walked away, protected your investment, moved on to the next opportunity." I turned in my seat to look at him properly. "But you didn't. You stayed. You believed in us. In GalvaTech and my family, even after everything with Parker. That means more to me than I can say."

He reached across the console and threaded his fingers through mine. "I stayed because I believe in the product. The charger is going to be revolutionary." He glanced at me, his expression tender. "And I stayed because I love you. Your dreams are my dreams now, Morgan. Your family is my family. This company matters to you, so it matters to me."

My throat tightened with emotion. "How did I get so lucky?"

"Pretty sure I'm the lucky one." He brought my hand to his lips and kissed the back of it. "You put up with me and my workaholic habits. You forgive me when I screw up. You challenge me to be better." His voice dropped lower. "And you love me anyway."

"I do love you," I said softly. "So much it scares me sometimes."

He arched a brow. "Good scared or bad scared?"

"Good scared. The kind that means it's real. That what we have matters."

"Agreed," he said, smiling at me.

We arrived at the gallery, and Liam found a parking spot near the entrance. Before we got out, he turned to me.

"Are you nervous about meeting Noah and Fallon, and the rest of my family?"

"A little," I admitted. "I want them to like me."

"They're going to love you as much as I do." He cupped my cheek, his thumb stroking my skin. "How could they not?"

I rolled my eyes. "You're biased."

"Maybe, but I'm also right." He leaned in and kissed me softly. "Come on. Let's go admire some art and introduce you to my family."

The art show had just opened when we arrived, but the gallery was already packed. The space was divided into four large, open rooms with white walls and light wooden floors, a perfect blank canvas for displaying art. Amazing paintings hung on every wall, and several large pieces on easels sat in the center of each room.

According to Liam, Fallon's work had been Pop Art for years but she'd recently expanded into landscapes, animals, and people. I admired her bold use of color and found myself drawn to a stunning painting of a mother and baby elephant playing in a river.

"She's quite talented," I said to Liam, but the person who responded was a woman to my left.

"That's nice to hear," she said, giving me a friendly smile. She was pretty with dark hair. "And it's nice to meet Liam's girlfriend."

I held out my hand. "You must be Fallon. I'm Morgan."

"You're Morgan?" an older woman exclaimed, rushing up to us while Fallon shook my hand. She had brown hair streaked with gray and excitement danced in her eyes. "I've been dying to meet the woman who's thawed my son's frozen heart."

"Oh my God, Mom." Liam groaned, and I laughed. "Can you play it just a little cool?"

"Absolutely not," she said cheerfully. Then she proved it by pulling me into a hug the moment Fallon released my hand.

Her embrace was warm, and she smelled like vanilla. I liked her immediately.

"Be nice to your mother," I chided Liam when she released me.

"Oh, I like her," his mom said, beaming. "Come along, Morgan. I'll introduce you to the rest of the family."

She looped her arm through mine and steered me through the crowd until we reached a small group standing near a large canvas of a laughing woman. I met Liam's brother Noah, who'd brought his adorable twin daughters to support his wife. The girls were excited to be there, and I learned they took art classes that Fallon taught at the gallery. Simon joined our group a few minutes later with a pretty woman by his side—Liam's younger sister, Shannon.

We all moved through the gallery together, looking at the paintings, and I hit it off with Shannon immediately. She was funny and interesting, and I told her that.

"You're right." She grinned. "You'll learn just how much fun I am once we go out to a bar together."

"Hey, don't corrupt my woman," Liam protested.

"I would never," Shannon said with wide-eyed innocence I didn't buy for a second.

"Come on. Let's break away from the group for a while so I can have you to myself for a bit." Liam grabbed my hand and pulled me toward the back of the gallery, where a painting of a flock of birds in flight during a sunset took up half the wall.

"This one's my favorite," he said as we stopped in front of it.

I leaned into him, studying the painting. I could see why he was fond of it. "It's beautiful. The way she captured the movement, you can almost feel them flying."

"That's what I love about it." His arm slipped around my waist. "It reminds me of how I felt when I finally let myself fall for you. Like I'd been caged for years and suddenly, I could breathe again."

I turned to look up at him, warmth spreading through me. "That's pretty poetic for an investment guy."

"You bring it out in me." His smile was soft and

genuine. "I spent so long convinced I was better off alone. That relationships were a complication I didn't want or need." He brushed a strand of hair behind my ear. "Then you walked into my life and turned everything upside down."

"I seem to remember you being pretty resistant at first," I teased him.

"Terrified is more accurate, but look at us now," he said, his thumb gently tracing my cheekbone. "My family already adores you, by the way. Did you see my mom's face? I thought she was going to start planning our wedding right there in the gallery."

I laughed. "She seems wonderful. They all do." I grew more serious, meeting his gaze and holding it. "You know, I'm really glad you ditched your brother's wedding reception the night we met."

"I guess some things are meant to be." He tilted my chin up and kissed me softly, tenderly, a promise sealed with his lips.

When we pulled apart, I smiled at him, feeling more content than I'd ever been.

I liked the sound of that. *Meant to be.* Because standing here with him, surrounded by art and his family and possibilities, I'd never been more certain of anything in my life.

Liam was my future, and I couldn't wait to spend every moment of it with him.

EPILOGUE

Liam

Nine Months Later

TODAY WAS MORGAN'S birthday. Which meant it had been exactly one year since the day we met. There was a lot to celebrate.

I'd gotten pretty good at spoiling my girl over the past year, but I wanted to plan something special for today. She was out to dinner with her friends—a birthday tradition, apparently—but I was meeting up with her afterward at the same bar where we'd first met.

While I waited, I ordered a drink from the bartender and checked my phone to see a text from Parker.

Heading home for the night. See you tomorrow.

I smiled and sent back a quick confirmation. Parker had been out of rehab for two weeks now and was back at GalvaTech, but we had strict protocols in place. A probationary period where his computer activity was monitored, random drug tests were given, and he checked in with me via text when he left the office each day. He also had mandatory meetings at NA that he had to attend daily, at least initially.

It was decided I should be the one he reported to instead of his stepfather. There'd been a lot of rebuilding of trust in the family over the past nine months, and Samuel didn't think it would be healthy for their relationship if he had to be the one keeping a close eye on Parker.

I honestly didn't mind. I was proud of Parker. He'd worked his ass off to get clean and stay that way. For Becca. For Gracie. For their son, Adam.

I tucked my phone away just as the bar door opened and Morgan walked in. I'd arranged for Whitney to drop her off, so she was alone as she strolled to the bar, giving me a moment to look her over.

We lived together now, but I wasn't home when she left for dinner, so I didn't see what dress she'd decided to wear. It was a deep red color and cut low in front, exposing a lot of cleavage and making my mouth go dry as I watched her breasts bounce with each step. The hem came to around mid-thigh, and her black boots reached her knees, leaving just a glimpse of smooth, tanned leg. Enough to make my dick twitch in my pants and ignite my desire for her.

She walked to the bar without looking at me, even though she came to stand right next to where I sat. I grinned and made no effort to hide the fact that I was staring as she caught the bartender's attention and ordered a Sex on the Beach, the same drink I'd bought her a year ago.

When he handed it over, she opened her little black clutch and frowned. "Oh, no." Her voice was perfectly distressed. If I didn't know her so well, I might have bought it. "I can't find my credit card."

"How about I buy your drink for you?" I suggested with a wolfish grin.

This whole recreation of our first meeting had been my idea, but the spark of excitement in her eyes told me Morgan was loving every second of it.

"I don't know," she said, biting her bottom lip. "I don't usually accept drinks from strangers."

I held out my hand. "I'm Liam."

"Morgan." She placed her hand in mine.

I brought it to my lips, brushing a soft kiss across her knuckles. Even after a year together, the connection between us still sizzled.

"Now we're not strangers," I said, my voice dropping lower.

"I suppose I can accept your offer then." She slid onto the stool beside mine, taking a sip of her drink while I signaled the bartender to put it on my tab. "So, what do you do when you're not hanging around in bars buying drinks for random women?"

I sipped my bourbon, keeping my eyes on her over the rim of my glass. "I own a company that invests in other businesses."

She grinned. "Does that mean you go in and start bossing people around? That must drive everyone crazy."

I smirked. "The women seem to like my bossy ways." Especially her.

She arched one perfect eyebrow. "Oh, really?"

"Really." I leaned closer, lowering my voice so only she could hear. "Just yesterday, I had a sexy as fuck woman bent over her own desk, stifling her cries of pleasure so the whole office wouldn't figure out what I was doing to her."

Her breath hitched and that lovely blush of hers swept across her cheeks. I watched her pupils dilate as she relived that particular afternoon. Completely unprofessional and definitely a risk to have sex at the office, but I knew that just turned her on more. We broke that particular rule at least once a week, sometimes in my office, sometimes in hers. I was still splitting my time between my own company and GalvaTech and, I had to say, I loved the convenience of having Morgan right next door.

"Sounds like a lucky woman," she managed.

"Trust me, I'm the lucky one."

We continued the flirty banter as we finished our drinks, falling back into the rhythm of that first night. The chemistry that had sparked between us immediately was still alive and well. The way conversation flowed so easily despite the heat and awareness simmering underneath.

"So, what brings you out tonight?" I asked, placing my empty glass on the bar. "Any special occasion?"

Her eyes lit up. "Actually, it's my birthday."

I grinned and leaned closer, running my fingers

over the back of her hand. "And do you have a birthday wish?"

She pretended to think about it, tapping one finger against her lips. "If I could have anything for my birthday…" She met my eyes, and the playfulness shifted into something deeper, more real. "I think I'd like to spend the night with you."

She put just the right amount of sweetness in her voice to make it feel authentic, and desire slammed through me. This woman. God, she drove me absolutely crazy in all the best ways.

"Let's get out of here." I signaled the bartender to cash out my tab. "I know of a hotel nearby."

"How convenient," she murmured with a knowing smile.

Anticipation quickened my pulse as I took her hand and led her across the street. I'd already checked into the room earlier, so we headed straight for the elevator.

Of course it was the same suite as last time. But I'd made it special for tonight.

I let Morgan enter first, watching her face as she took in the rose petals scattered across the bed, the champagne chilling in a bucket of ice next to a slice of chocolate cake, and the flameless candles flickering throughout the room.

"Liam," she breathed, turning back to me.

She gasped when she saw that I was already down on one knee, holding a black velvet ring box. The time for role-playing was over. I opened the box to reveal a princess cut diamond on a white gold band. My hands were steadier than I expected, but my heart was racing.

"Morgan Starling." My voice came out rough with emotion. "I can't believe how much you've changed my life this past year. I never thought I'd be brave enough to love again until you came along and knocked down all my walls. You made me realize that real love is impossible to resist. More than that, I don't want to. Because loving you makes me happier than I've ever been, happier than I knew I could be."

Tears glistened in her eyes, but her expression was radiant.

"You're my best friend. My partner. The person I want to come home to every single day for the rest of my life." I took a breath. "Will you marry me?"

"Yes." She nodded, laughing and crying at the same time as she held out her hand. "Yes, of course I will."

My heart felt like it would burst from happiness as I slid the ring onto her finger. The fit was perfect. I'd used one of her other rings weeks ago to get the size just right.

I surged to my feet and pulled her into my arms, kissing her like my life depended on it. She wrapped her arms around my neck, kissing me back with equal intensity.

"I love you, Liam Powers," she whispered against my lips. "So much."

"I love you too, baby." I swept her up and carried her toward the bed. "And I'm going to spend the rest of the night showing you exactly how much."

"The rest of the night?" Her eyes sparkled with mischief and desire. "That's all?"

I laid her down on the bed and covered her body with mine. "You're right. That's not nearly enough time."

"We have the rest of our lives," she said softly, cupping my face in her hands.

"The rest of our lives," I echoed, the words filling me with a contentment I'd never thought possible. "I love the sound of that."

Then I kissed my fiancée and showed her exactly how much I planned to enjoy every single moment of our future together.

Starting right now.

Thanks for reading! Up next is **JUST A LITTLE TEMPTED**, a story in Carly Phillips' Sterling Family world.

Other books in the Sterling Family Crossover Series:
JUST A LITTLE CRUSH
JUST A LITTLE TEMPTED

Other books in the Dare Crossover Bachelor Auction Series:
JUST A LITTLE HOOKUP
JUST A LITTLE SECRET
JUST A LITTLE PROMISE
JUST A LITTLE CHASE

For Book News:
SIGN UP for Carly's Newsletter:
carlyphillips.com/CPNewsletter
SIGN UP for Erika's Newsletter:
geni.us/ErikaWildeNewsletter

Carly Phillips and Erika Wilde Booklist

A Sterling Family Crossover Series

Just A Little Crush
Just A Little Desire
Just A Little Tempted

A Dare Crossover Series

Just A Little Hookup
Just A Little Secret
Just A Little Promise
Just A Little Chase

Dirty Sexy Series

Dirty Sexy Saint
Dirty Sexy Inked
Dirty Sexy Cuffed
Dirty Sexy Sinner

Book Boyfriend Series

Big Shot
Faking It
Well Built
Rock Solid

The Boyfriend Experience

About the Authors

CARLY PHILLIPS is the bestselling author of over eighty sexy contemporary romances featuring hot men, strong women, and the emotionally compelling stories her readers have come to expect and love. She is happily married to her college sweetheart and the mother of two adult daughters and their crazy dogs. She loves social media and is always around to interact with her readers. You can find out more and get two free books at www.carlyphillips.com.

ERIKA WILDE is the author of the sexy Marriage Diaries series and The Players Club series. She lives in Oregon with her husband and two daughters, and when she's not writing you can find her exploring the beautiful Pacific Northwest. For more information on her upcoming releases, please visit website at www.erikawilde.com.

Made in United States
North Haven, CT
18 December 2025